"You're a beautiful woman," Gallagher said

"And you don't need me to tell you that."

"No, I don't," Charlie agreed woodenly. Especially not now, she thought.

She was alone with him in isolation as intense as it got. She was feeling the aftereffects of both adrenaline and relief.

It would be too easy to give in to a purely physical celebration of the moment. To seek the warmth, the strength, the comfort, of his arms, his lips ... She forced her eyes away from those lips.

For the first time, probably for the only time, she had seen a vulnerable side to Gallagher. It was compelling. She slid away from the hands resting on her neck, suddenly too aware of how they offered not only comfort, but electrical promise. . . .

Quinn Wilder, a Canadian writer, was born and raised in Calgary, but now lives in the Okanagan Valley away from the bustle of a city. She has had a variety of jobs, but her favorite pastime has always been writing. She graduated from the Southern Alberta Institute of Technology Journalism Arts program in 1979. Since then she has free-lanced, and her list of credits includes magazine articles, educational material, scripts, speeches and so on. Her first novel became a Harlequin, marking a high point in her career. She enjoys skiing and horseback riding.

Books by Quinn Wilder

HARLEQUIN ROMANCE
2772—THAT MAN FROM TEXAS
2886—TO TAME A WILD HEART
2904—DAUGHTER OF THE STARS

HIGH
HEAVEN
Quinn Wilder

Harlequin Books

TORONTO • NEW YORK • LONDON
AMSTERDAM • PARIS • SYDNEY • HAMBURG
STOCKHOLM • ATHENS • TOKYO • MILAN

Original hardcover edition published in 1989
by Mills & Boon Limited

ISBN 0-373-03096-7

Harlequin Romance first edition December 1990

With many thanks to
Gord Jeffrey
who so generously and enthusiastically
shared his expertise
on helicopters
and the heli-skiing industry

CHAPTER ONE

GALLAGHER COLE tried to stare the woman down. When she did not flinch under the scathing scrutiny of his gaze, he felt his ire rise—higher, that was. He was already annoyed beyond belief. He had placed so many hopes in this candidate. That was why he'd saved this meeting for last. Because already in his mind, based on the recommendations of several people he'd thought were his friends, he had given the job to one Charlie James.

Now, as he skimmed rapidly through his mind over the other people he'd talked to, he realised that he'd interviewed them all with a subconscious lack of interest because he'd been so certain that Charlie would be the one for the job.

The helicopter industry was small and closed, and when he'd begun his enquiries that one name had come to him again and again. Charlie was an excellent pilot. Charlie had eighteen months' experience on the Bell 212. Charlie met the 'high time' requirement. Best of all, it was known that Charlie wanted out of the Beaufort Sea. He was willing to take less money for more time at home.

7

He. Ha, thought Gallagher blackly. How could he have had three separate conversations with old connections from helicopter companies and not have noticed something vaguely stilted about the rave reviews for Charlie James? Something like the complete absence of personal pronouns? Charlie this, Charlie that. Pilot this. Individual that. No he. No she. He felt very much like he'd been the victim of a conspiracy. And *she'd* been the ringleader, charming away loyalties he'd established when he'd worked in the oil patch.

Dammit. He was going to have to start again. But the problem was that he couldn't just be satisfied with competence. He wanted his passion and his enthusiasm for his company to be mirrored back at him. He thought he had read that potential in between each word of praise for Charlie James, and now he was seething at his own lack of businesslike behaviour, his own lack of foresight. He had to be ready to go in a few weeks. Damn Martin Mick to hell for leaving him stranded on such short notice.

The silence dragged, but he was preoccupied with his own thoughts, and not the least apologetic about his desire to make her feel uncomfortable. But it was only adding to the slow burn within him that she showed not a sign of discomfort—or the guilt he thought she should be showing.

A chill permeated the air of the tiny room at the back of the hangar that he used as an office.

If she was cold, she was too stubborn to shiver. If she was uncomfortable on the straight-backed wooden chair, she didn't show that either.

You would think, he told himself righteously, she'd have the decency to be nervous. But he knew that the chair on which she was seated had one leg shorter than the other. The slightest twitch would have sent it rocking—which it was not doing.

Though his eyes had never left her, he returned his full attention to her, studying her relentlessly. He admitted that she might have turned his head had he encountered her in different circumstances. Her hair was long and shimmering—gold-streaked, with strands that ranged from sun-kissed blonde, to honey-coloured brown. The hair was pulled rather severely off her face, neatly caught in a black ribbon at her nape. But somehow that ponytail had come over her shoulder, and was cascading over her breast, tangled and tawny, looking like liquid sunshine against the dreary backdrop of his office. Gallagher Cole prided himself on not having many weaknesses, but one of them was for deliciously long hair. The fact that some purely male portion of his brain was undoing that silken hair from the bondage of its ribbon served to push his anger a few notches higher.

A woman blessed with hair like that should, by some balancing law of nature, be cursed with a face as bland as bread dough.

But the fact was that she was definitely not

bland; and even that fact, as out of her control as it might be, managed to irritate him. It was the face of an angel regarding him with sombre composure. A strong face—high cheekbones, a square chin, wide, firm lips, a straight, proud nose. The face might have been almost too strong, save that it was tempered by large, soft-as-suede, golden brown eyes. Though the eyes that met his unblinkingly held a trace of steel, that steel was mingled with an intriguing hint of mystery. Maturity. Wisdom.

She was tall and slender, almost boyishly built. Her shoulders were wide, like those of a swimmer, her breasts a supple, enticing swell beneath a soft beige brushed-cotton shirt, her waist tiny, her hips non-existent, her legs long and coltish in a pair of beige, multi-pocketed canvas trousers.

She could have been—and should have been—a model, Gallagher deduced cynically. What she shouldn't have been, and wasn't going to be—at least, not for him—was a helicopter pilot.

'Miss James,' he finally growled, when she made no move to break the silence he had engineered, 'I feel as though I've been duped.' He watched her narrowly to see how she handled the blunt return of the ball to her court.

She did not flush. She did not squirm. She did not break her hold on his eyes.

'Why is that, Mr Cole?' she asked evenly. Her voice was splendid—husky, sensual, and yet natural. That was what was wrong with her, he thought—she seemed natural, unaware or uninterested in her own attractiveness. Which only made him feel more duped than ever.

'Let's not play games, Miss James,' he suggested tersely. 'I think you're probably aware that no one from Tundra, Sunrise or Bellview thought to mention to me that you were a woman. Frankly, I find your use of a man's name crafty and unconscionable.'

She returned his look, golden eyes unwavering, unflinching from the fact that he had obviously switched to hard ball. 'That happens to be my name, Mr Cole, so my use of it could hardly be seen as unscrupulous. And I'm sure that Wally, Bert and Harold only thought that your expectation would be to interview a helicopter pilot, which I am.'

'I think,' he narrowed his eyes at her, 'that it might have been ethical, at some point in our communication, for you to have indicated your gender.'

'Would I be sitting here if I had?' she returned, a hard note in her voice that matched his.

You most certainly would not be, thought Gallagher, but he said, 'That's hardly the point. With the help of your friends, you deliberately misled me. If your name is really Charlie, I'll eat my hat. I just don't believe that a deception makes a particularly good starting point for a working relationship, so let's just terminate——'

In one smooth movement she had got out of

her chair, swooped his baseball cap off its hook on the back of the door, and taken a document from her shirt pocket. She plunked both in front of him, a hint of fire blazing in those lioness eyes.

'Charles Cassandra James', the birth certificate read. Gallagher stared at it incredulously. 'Who the hell would name a girl Charles?' he pondered out loud.

'My grandfather died the night before I was born,' she supplied briefly. 'I don't appreciate being called a liar, Mr Cole. If I used my name to get my foot in the door, I consider that fair play. If some of my industry connections thought enough of my ability to want to see me at least have a shot at this position, that's also fair play. What is not fair play—and is also against the law in this country—is sexual discrimination.'

Gallagher did not particularly appreciate having the law shoved in his face, or being forced to have a look at his own prejudices. He had always, quite sincerely, believed that he didn't have any prejudices. He thought he believed in total equality for women. He had three sisters, after all! And he would be fighting mad if any of them had been turned down for a job because of her sex. But then they'd all had the sense to choose jobs they were suited for. He was suddenly uncomfortably aware of the fact that he would not choose a woman doctor, and would not want to board a plane with a woman pilot, even if it was one of his sisters. And he most certainly did not want a woman flying a piece of his machinery that was worth a million dollars.

'OK,' he admitted grudgingly, 'maybe I am a bit of a dinosaur, but I'm simply uncomfortable with the notion of a woman flying a helicopter.' He refrained, just barely, from adding, Especially *my* helicopter.

'Why is that, Mr Cole?' For all that her tone was reasonable, there was no mistaking a warrior-like spark in her eyes.

This was no hollow-headed blonde interested in only her fingernails, her hair and her plans for Friday night, Gallagher conceded. Not that he had a thing against hollow-headed blondes. In fact, that seemed to be exactly what his taste ran to since Synthia. And, even though he found Charlie's no-nonsense attitude less than appealing, she was still an attractive woman. He was not at all sure that an attractive woman and a normal, healthy man could work together as intensively as they would have to and still maintain a strictly professional relationship.

'Why is that, Mr Cole?' she asked again.

He supposed that, if he told her about the birds and the bees, he would get slugged for his trouble.

'Look, Miss James, I believe in equal pay for equal work. I believe in equal opportunity—if we're talking about teaching. But I think there's a reality underlying the best-intentioned philosophies, and that's that men and women *are* different. They're raised differently, and with different perceptions and expectations of life. And, in my experience, women don't handle crises well. They start looking around for help as soon as the chips are down. This is a very high-pressure kind of flying——'

'I'm aware of the unique perils of heli-skiing,' she interjected, her tone strained with irritation. 'And I wouldn't be sitting here right now if I was the kind who panicked easily or looked around for help. I'd be dead.'

'Well, then, you're a different kind of woman from any I've ever met.'

'I have very little doubt about that,' she stated emphatically.

Gallagher sighed wearily. The decision was already irrevocably made in his mind. He didn't care if it was narrow-minded. Unfair. Archaic. It was his business, and he would run it how he pleased. Still, he supposed they were going to have to play this out until the end. He had no doubt that she was just the type who would have him in court on discrimination charges if he didn't make a damned good show of going through the motions.

'How old are you?'

'Twenty-eight.'

He whistled. 'You don't look a day over eighteen.' It slipped out, but he wasn't sorry. It was true, and there was no harm in flattering her, either—particularly if it meant staying out of court.

Except that she did not take his compliment as a peace offering. She regarded him coolly. 'Why is it, Mr Cole, that a woman is supposed to be delighted to be told she looks like a child? I'm twenty-eight years old. I enjoy being twenty-eight. I have no wish to be anything else.'

He glared at her. Hell, but she was touchy. He patted himself on the back for having known instantly and instinctively that he did not want to work with this woman. He conducted the rest of the interview with stiff formality, trying very hard to keep his sense of justification alive in light of the confidence and clarity of her answers.

Finally, secure in the knowledge that he had given her just about the best interview ever given, he began to wrap it up.

'Revelstoke is a very small community. Some might even call it boring.' He never had, but some might. 'I think this job would really be more suited to someone with a family, who would want to settle here, make a contribution to the community and the economy.'

'Actually, I do want to settle in a small community.' A wistful sincerity crept into that no-nonsense tone. 'I like the idea of people knowing my name. I like the idea of a place that's cleaner and safer and more easygoing. I don't think a big city is a good place for . . . for family.'

Gallagher frowned. Family? That was precisely what was wrong with all these rules and regulations governing what you were allowed to ask people. Well, he didn't have to ask to find out.

'I didn't realise you were married.'

'I'm not.'

Aha, Gallagher thought with cool satisfaction. A woman interested in a family who didn't have a husband. No wonder his warning lights had been flashing crimson since she had strode through the door. She was searching for a husband. And husband-hunters had a terrible tendency to latch on to him.

'I have a dependant,' she said with soft hesitation.

Far from softening him, the news that she had a child hardened him even more. She would *really* be searching for a husband. Maybe she'd assumed heli-skiing attracted some very wealthy men, which it did. But damned if his business was going to be used for a marital shopping-ground!

It momentarily pricked his conscience that if she had a child she probably really needed a job. Well, tough! She should have kept the one she had had in the Beaufort. Except that she probably wanted to be with her kid. He felt sorry about that. Briefly. And not sorry enough to even consider giving her the job.

'I think that's about everything. I've got a number of people I want to talk to, Miss James, so why don't I let you know? I'll call you in Calgary in a week, either way.'

He saw something flicker in her eyes and was mildly ashamed of himself. She knew she was being brushed off.

'Aren't you going to let me fly?'

The 'absolutely not' died in his throat. She had shown herself to be a proud woman, and yet there was faint pleading in those magnificent eyes.

He glanced outside. It was a beautiful, clear mountain day. Leon, his other pilot, had already been up, so the helicopter was ready to go. He didn't have to let her do anything but go up and come down. He sighed, and then shrugged. What the heck? 'OK. We'll go for a spin.'

They walked past several small planes that he shared the hangar with.

He couldn't help but notice that she looked at them with *that* look in her eyes. He didn't want to identify the look, but he did anyway. It was a pilot's look. The look of one who loved flying and flying machines.

The look in her eyes intensified as they came out of the back door, and to his helicopter. It was a Bell 212, affectionately referred to as a Twin Huey, and her face showed complete reverence. He felt the indifference he wanted to feel for her slip a bit. She so obviously appreciated this machine that represented his dream. Its sleek lines, the custom paint job, the words he hoped would become legend embossed across the side in heavy gold letters. 'High Heaven Heli-Ski'. She turned to him and gave him a dazzling smile that made her extraordinarily beautiful, and erased the no-nonsense, almost militant countenance she had presented in his office.

And then he knew he was forgotten. He watched her circle the helicopter, carrying out the rather extensive exterior check. She finally nodded her satisfaction and stepped up to the door. He did the same. She did her interior check, then took her seat and belted herself in. Her brow was knitted in calm concentration; she was completely engrossed as she placed the helmet over her head and began the engine pre-start checks.

Finally, she opened the engine throttles, and a few minutes later they were airborne. Gallagher was one of those people who found it impossible to rub his stomach and pat his head at the same time. He admired the dexterity of helicopter pilots. Getting these birds off the ground and flying them meant that each limb was doing a different task at the same time—hands working the collective and cyclic controls, feet adding and subtracting torque with pedals on the floor. He was glad, and not for the first time, that he was not involved in the complex business of flying this machine. Then he reminded himself sternly that he was supposed to be fearing for his life, not giving this particular pilot his confidence.

He adjusted his headset, and directed her gruffly to go over the peaks of Mount Begbie. He watched her appraisingly for a while. Her face was expressionless, save for that look of calm confidence. She flew with a skill that looked deceptively effortless, with a finesse he knew he could expect from a pilot with five thousand hours, and yet had not expected from her. Without even being aware of it, he stopped paying attention to her, feeling the ease in his gut that he always felt in these mountains that surrounded his home. They soared towards brilliant snow-capped mountains, swooped over the peaks and down in the valleys.

'Where do you ski?'

So much for going up and coming down, he thought. But since they were up, he might as well check out the areas of the Monashee and Selkirk ranges that he had exclusive guiding rights to. He gave her directions, and before he knew it he had given in to the temptation to check most of the fifteen hundred square miles of slopes that, in a month, he would be leading skiers down. There was still some rock showing, he noticed, but soon . . .

'Do you want me to put her down?'

'No. Not today.' The words startled him. Not today? Not any day, Charlie James. But it was a lie, and he knew it. She was good, very good, considering how intensely critical he had intended to be of her skill, and how quickly he had forgotten all about who was flying.

He suspected that she knew he was reluctantly impressed, because she flashed him a grin that held leprechaun mischievousness and made her look about sixteen—not that he would have dared to say it.

Once back on the ground, they sat in a silence that seemed more pronounced without the steady, distinctive 'wop' of the single rotor system helicopter.

'This is such a beautiful place,' she finally murmured. Like him, she was looking out across the narrow valley of the landing strip towards the soaring white caps of Mount Begbie.

He nodded his agreement, her genuine appreciation loosening something inside him. 'I was born here. Raised here. I've been in every corner of the world since, but I always come home. You'll find that about Revelstoke. Families have been here for generations. There are people who have never left, and don't feel like they've missed anything. On days like this one, I find myself agreeing. Those who do leave, like me, always seem to find their way back to this little piece of heaven.'

'Is that where the name came from?'

'The name?'

'High Heaven?'

'No. The name came from what's up there.' His gaze moved back towards the peaks, his voice unconsciously softened. 'It's something to see on a crisp mountain morning. The snow lies thick and silent on the mountain, the air is pure, the sky is as blue as you'll ever see that colour. The valleys are often lost in cloud, so you have a sense of being isolated in this world of endless snow, hissing skis, waist-high powder. That world, the one up there, seems much, much closer to heaven than it does to this world down here.' He smiled. 'My grandmother wasn't a woman who was easily impressed, but about twice a year some monumental event, like her favourite wrestler winning a match, would move her to say, ''Well, praise to high heaven.'' As a little boy I used to take her very literally and try to figure out what high heaven looked like. The first time I ski'd the deep powder, I felt a sense of recognition. ''Ah, so this is it.'''

Charlie laughed, and it was a deep, rich sound. 'Come to think of it, my grandma used to use that term, too, only in quite a different context. When my Aunt Joss was cooking cabbage soup, Grandma would say, ''Goodness gracious, it stinks to high heaven in here!'''

Gallagher grimaced. 'That's hardly the association I'm looking for. Do you ski?'

A barely perceptible shadow crossed her face. 'I used to. A long time ago.' She smiled, a wistfulness in her eyes. 'Time and money ran out at about the same time.'

Something in her expression made him feel that there was more to it than that—that something had caused her to let go of the frivolous adventures of youth too young. 'My pilots fly the standard two weeks on, two off schedule. If there's an empty seat, and they want to ski, they're always welcome.'

'Does that mean I'm going to be one of your pilots?' she queried softly, and he could tell that, for the first time, she was losing some of that composure, for she was trying very hard not to sound too eager.

He took off his hat, ran his fingers through his hair. 'On one condition.'

'What's that?'

He passed her the cap. 'That you'll wear this, instead of holding me to eating it.'

She stared down at the hat, tracing her fingers over the embossed gold lettering that read 'High Heaven'.

Her eyes sparkled with tears, and he thought, Oh, sure—now that you've got the job, fall apart and act like a woman.

But the tears that shone in her eyes never fell. She plunked the cap on her head, then turned and gave him a brilliant smile. 'You've got yourself a deal, Mr Cole.'

'Gallagher,' he corrected gruffly. How many women's beauty would be accentuated by a duck-billed baseball cap? But the cap, by its very masculinity, made him aware that she possessed her own brand of very potent femininity. It made him a trifle uneasy that she looked so proud to be wearing that hat, and that it looked so good on her—as if she had been born to wear it.

Syn, too, had looked like she was born to wear caps and ski toques, though that was where the resemblance between her and Charlie would end. Not that Syn had been one of these brazen blondes he always seemed to have clutching his

arm these days, either. Syn had been small and
delicate and so utterly gentle. Nothing at all like
this self-possessed young woman who flew
helicopters.

He watched Charlie come around the
helicopter towards him on those long legs, and
wondered uneasily what he had got himself into.
Nothing, he answered himself. His choices had
been limited. He was pressed for time; she was a
good pilot. If it proved to be a mistake, then he
would replace her. It was that simple. One slip
and Charlie James would be history, particularly
if she got ideas about invading his personal life.
Not that he had much to give to a personal life.
High Heaven took it all, and there hadn't been a
woman yet who didn't tire of its endless
demands, the time it took, his preoccupation
with it. There had been many who had tried.
They'd been left cold when they had started
whining for more of him than he'd been
prepared to give. And so would Charlie James, if
she started flitting those dark, tangled lashes in
his direction. She would be left cold . . . and
jobless. He made a mental note to keep himself
updated on what was available in the way of
pilots. He wouldn't be caught in a bind again.

'Our first trip is booked for a month from
now.' Gallagher deliberately reinstated a
businesslike chill to his voice. 'I'd like you to be
here a week early for the staff orientation.'

'I'll be here,' she promised. 'Mr
Cole—Gallagher—thank you.'

He shrugged. 'You're a damn good pilot.'

She gave him that leprechaun grin again. 'I know.'

He watched her walk away and get into an old wreck of a Pontiac. It took two or three starts for her to get the engine going, and then she gave him a jaunty wave and drove away.

If he had trouble accepting a woman in the world of flying, he wondered, how would his conservative, mostly male, and heavily European clientele react? That woman had probably just set herself up for a walk through hell. How would she handle someone refusing to fly with her? How would she handle the invariable passes that would be made at her? It occurred to him that she had probably handled all those situations before. His real worry was how *he* would handle it.

'See?' He spoke out loud. 'The trouble is already starting.' He wouldn't be standing out here talking to himself if he'd hired a man.

'You've really done it now!' he told the empty road warningly, and then turned and walked away.

CHAPTER TWO

CHARLIE was no sooner out of sight of the hangar, than she pulled the car over to the side of the road and laid her head against the steering wheel. Her composure had been threatened to breaking point more than once in her meeting with Gallagher Cole, and now it broke. She took several deep, steadying breaths.

She felt exhausted and giddy. She wanted to get out of the car and do a mad little jig in the middle of the highway. She had a job! She had taken a chance, and won!

But she knew she had come close to blowing it, and she berated herself for her temper. What on earth had possessed her to lecture him after his unthinking remark about her age? The man had put her back up, there was no doubt about that, but what if he was back in his office right now, trying to think of ways to get out of having offered her the job? He would be thinking it over, wondering why he had hired such a shrew . . .

She touched the brim of the cap she was still wearing, and her worries dissipated, the thrill swept over her again. Sighing happily, she pulled back on to the road, going over every word of the interview in her mind.

She chuckled as she recalled his face when
he'd looked down at her birth certificate.
'Thanks, Gramps,' she murmured, and it
occurred to her that she had never before been
grateful for her unusual name. If anything, she
had rather thought her grandfather's demise on
the eve of her birth had been an omen of the life
to come.

'Stop,' she ordered herself firmly. Now was
not the time to start questioning why her life
seemed so much more difficult than anyone
else's. Now was the time to look forward to
starting again, to allow herself to hope that
finally she had left betrayal and loss and sadness
behind her. Besides, there was nothing left to
lose. It had all been taken from her already. Her
mother and father had left her with an aunt and
uncle when she was small, and had hardly
looked back. Aunt Joss had been dead for seven
years, Uncle Henry, six. Paul, and the Cinderella
visions he'd left in tatters, were far behind her
now. It was all far behind her. She was starting
afresh—her and Kenny.

She smiled, the smile unconsciously winsome.
Yes, there was still Kenny. There would always
be Kenny. She wondered if she should call him.
There probably wasn't much point. He wouldn't
really understand, anyway. On the other hand,
she wanted to share this triumph with someone,
and he was the only one. For a moment she felt
an almost crushing sense of loneliness, but she

pushed it firmly away. It did not belong in this day. And, after all these years of coping and being strong, today was not the day to let self-pity catch up with her.

She called her home in Calgary as soon as she was back in her hotel room. The housekeeper answered.

'Did you get the job?' she was asked crisply.

'Yes!'

'Humph. I suppose that means my job is over.'

'I suppose it does,' Charlie said, unable to feign regret.

'Well, I can't say as I'm overly sorry. Your cousin is a singularly difficult young man. Not that it's his fault, his being a simpleton and all.'

Charlie felt her temper rise. How dared she call Kenny a simpleton?

'The term is mentally handicapped, if we must use labels at all,' Charlie informed Mrs Jones tersely, and not for the first time.

'In my mind, his problem isn't a lack of brain, at any rate,' Charlie was informed coldly. 'It's that he's spoiled and wilful. Given his size and his strength, that could lead to real trouble, unless you take matters in hand. It's not as if we're talking about a boy, after all.'

White-hot fury surged through Charlie. She hated the stereotypes, the entrenched myths that surrounded her cousin's handicap. As if Kenny were somehow dangerous, or would become dangerous. Kenny, who was gentle and mild, and childlike for all his twenty-two years. OK, so he did like to have his own way. OK, so she was guilty of giving into him entirely too much. Sometimes, with all of life's little pressures, it was just so easy to choose the path of least resistance when it came to her cousin. But Kenny wasn't dangerous, and never would be.

She let her eyes wander out of her hotel-room to the sleepy streets of Revelstoke. New beginnings, she reminded herself. Maybe it wasn't going to be so hard here. Maybe, in this smaller, more closely knit community, people would be more willing to get to know Kenny for who he was, instead of shying away from his handicap. She hoped so. She had just staked her future on it.

Kenny came on to the line. 'Chuck? Chuckie? I hate Mrs Jones. I hate her. Come home! I miss you.'

Charlie smiled wryly at the deep voice and the childlike words. Kenny. Oh, beautiful Kenny. The tall, handsome young man with the chiselled features and bronze hair. With the large, innocently rounded eyes of a child.

'I miss you, too, love. But I can't come home for a few days. I got the job, Kenny.'

'The job, Chuckie?'

She sighed. She had explained it so carefully and thoroughly before she had come here.

'The job flying a helicopter for people who like to ski, Kenny. Remember?'

'Can I go in the helicopter, Chuckie? Please, please, please?'

'We'll have to see, Kenny.'

'I want to go in the helicopter,' Kenny wailed.

'I said we'll see.' She changed the subject hurriedly. 'We'll be moving here, Kenny. I'll tell you all about it when I get home. I think you'll like it.'

'I don't want to move,' he informed her stubbornly.

'I won't have to go away overnight any more.'

'Oh. Can I have a dog there?'

'No!'

'Will we have an elevator where we live? I like elevators.'

Charlie looked out at the low buildings of Revelstoke. She highly doubted there was an elevator in the whole town. 'Kenny, I'll be home in a few days. We'll talk about it then, OK?'

'Don't hang up, Chuckie,' he pleaded. 'Come home right now!' He was starting to cry. 'Mrs Jones is mean. She hates me. I never have any fun.'

'I have to go, Kenny,' she interrupted quietly. 'I'll be home soon. I'll bring you a present. Be good.' She gently replaced the receiver on his sobbing shriek.

The 'Chuck-eee' was still ringing in her ears as she walked over to the window and gazed out. She was feeling blue, and she knew she had no one to blame but herself. She shouldn't have called. The scene in front of her eventually

pierced her gloom. Revelstoke looked like a
picture from a Christmas card. The streets were
quiet, golden lights flickering from behind the
windows of marvellous old houses. In the
background, visible even through the lacy
curtain of falling snow, loomed the mountains.

What was it, she wondered, about these huge
monuments of rock and tree, and snow-capped
peaks, that so touched the souls of mere
mortals? Whatever it was, it soothed her now.
There was a serenity in the scene that made it
easier to get Kenny's heart-wrenching wail into
perspective. She was here to build a life for him.
If he had to spend a few more unhappy days
while she ironed out the details, then that was
the price, and they had to pay it. For the last
time. She felt enormous relief that those
agonising two-week partings, which they'd
experienced over and over again when she'd
worked in the Beaufort, were over.

Without warning her mind drifted to
Gallagher Cole, and her new-found serenity
became edged with a fine tension. Hell, but he
was an attractive devil, a stunning specimen of
masculinity.

He had the type of face that was intriguing to
look at, the type of face that you wanted to look
at again and again, as if each glance might reveal
some new and tantalising dimension to him. His
eyes were the most amazing shade of dark blue,
fringed with an abundance of thick black lashes.
In a little over an hour she had seen hints of a

very complex man in those eyes.

She shivered slightly, remembering how intimidating those eyes had been in his anger. His narrowed gaze had been electrical, overwhelmingly forceful. She was a little astonished by the façade of cool composure she had managed. And then, briefly, when he'd talked about skiing, and his grandmother, of all things, a warmth had touched the stone-coldness of those eyes, and he had become as compelling as he had been intimidating. But that moment had been very brief, and brought on, she suspected, by his empathy for the awesome magnificence of the land they had flown over.

She supposed he was handsome, and, in fact, he carried himself with the haughty self-assurance of one who was well aware of his appeal. And yet, for all that his eyes—sapphire against the deep bronze of his skin—and the perfect sculpt of his face, with its high cheekbones, straight nose and jutting chin, should have made him handsome, she was not left with an impression of handsomeness. His face had none of the bland perfection she usually associated with that word. His exposure to elements like wind and sun on snow had left his skin craggy and weather-beaten. His nose had been broken, and was faintly lopsided, and a white-ridged, jagged scar ran the length of his jawline, from his ear to his chin. But, rather than detracting, his imperfections intrigued, giving him a look that would have sat well on the face of a devil-may-care buccaneer laughing into the teeth of a storm. They gave him character, a look of hard determination, a look that suggested the confidence of command. A look that said strength, pure and simple.

That impression of rugged strength was emphasised again in his height, in the way he carried himself with the smooth and liquid grace of a magnificently conditioned athlete. There was a hard leanness about him—a thoroughbred sleekness, that had not been hidden in the least by his baggy 'High Heaven' embossed sweatshirt, and that had been all too evident in the moulded fit of his Levis.

She was pretty sure that Gallagher Cole would be the type of man who would have women throwing themselves at his size-eleven feet. And pretty sure that he was the kind that would stomp all over hearts with pleasure. Well, he was a physically enticing specimen, no two ways about it. And there was an arresting quality in that hard face that might tempt a woman to see if she could be the one who could soften him, tame him.

But Charlie felt no such temptation. She had survived—no, excelled—in a male-dominated profession because she was able to draw firm lines over which she never crossed. She had learned very early that, if she expected to be treated like a professional and accepted as a professional, her first rule of conduct must be *never* to get involved personally with the men she worked with. She was adept now at turning down dates—and more serious propositions—with a knack that left no hurt feelings, and that paved the way for her acceptance as 'just one of the guys'.

Yes, she would be able to handle Gallagher Cole. His attitudes about women belonged in a different century, and that alone was enough, thank heaven, to kill the physical appeal which there was no denying he had.

She only hoped he had the good sense not to complicate both their lives by seeing her as a challenge on a personal level. She knew from experience that her very aloofness sometimes goaded the male ego into seeing her as the ultimate conquest.

And Charlie's aloofness was not a game she played. It was earned. Hard-earned. She knew the price of letting people in. Every single person she had dared to love was gone now. A heart could only take so much in a single lifetime, and her heart had been pushed to its limit a long time ago. The exception was Kenny. And Kenny took all the love she had to give. There was none left over.

OK, occasionally, in a moment of weakness, she did wish for something more. But she wasn't even sure what it was—a wistful wisp of a wish for something magical to happen to her. Perhaps it was the lack of romance in her life that she felt, but she tended to think it didn't exist anyway, except in the pages of soppy stories that she refused to allow herself to read.

Right now she stood on the brink of having all she knew she should expect of life. She was too old to believe in fairy-tales, too jaded to be searching for a prince. Contentment should be enough, and she should have that with this regular and well-paying job. Kenny's future would be secure. She should be only thankful that she was able to do that by pursuing a career that she loved. Thankful that she was going to be able to make a home for him in this lovely, clean, quiet and safe community.

Romance was overrated. From her experience, it started off feeling wonderful, and ended up meaning nothing but trouble and heartache. Eventually, Kenny had to be considered within the context of any relationship she formed.

'Look, it's Kenny or me,' Paul had said.

Her first obligation then, her first obligation now, was to Kenny. There hadn't really been a choice. But it had still felt like she was making one, and it had still torn her apart inside.

She knew she had no right to be bitter about Paul's ultimatum. She knew it hadn't been fair to ask a man eager to start his own family to take on the burden of Kenny. She knew Paul had only been honest about his own limitations. But she could never quite dismiss the feeling that, if he had loved her enough . . .

She knew, now, that Paul's reaction had been a typical one. She had dated other men since Paul had disappeared from her life. As soon as it had become apparent that she and Kenny came part and parcel, interest in her had waned. And it had always hurt. She was bound to Kenny. She did not need the fresh pain of making an old decision over and over again. It had been over three years, now, since she had encouraged any kind of relationship. She accepted that that was how life was. Sometimes, she would meet a man who made her feel a moment's regret, which she hard-heartedly snuffed. A moment's regret now was better than a bucketful of tears later.

Gallagher Cole was not one of those men who made her feel regret, anyway. It was purely coincidence that these thoughts followed so closely on the heels of having met him.

Gallagher Cole. Kenny. What would Gallagher make of a request to take Kenny up on one of those days when they weren't flying full. What would a man like Gallagher make of Kenny, full stop?

The thought made her shiver. She was tired of leaving herself and Kenny open to the sting of other people's judgements, and Gallagher was ruthlessly judgemental, even if he had managed to overcome it this once. No, it would be better to keep her life in neat compartments. A personal one. A professional one. Kenny would not be flying—but then he would not be subjected to Gallagher Cole, either.

Kenny was wide-eyed with awe. 'Gee, look at the snow, Chuckie.'

Charlie *was* looking at the snow. She couldn't believe it. In the three short weeks since she had been there last, Revelstoke had turned into a winter wonderland. Before, there had been a faint dusting of snow covering the town and surrounding mountains, but now it was astonishingly deep. The paths were beginning to look like tunnels, with the snow banked high on either side. She now understood that the strange sandwich-boards which she had noticed over tiny trees and shrubs protected them from the tremendous weight of snow. The house that she had rented was completely surrounded with heaps that had been sliding off the slippery metal roof. The snow was touching the window-sills. Kenny and Charlie both jumped as a huge slice broke from the roof, hissed down the metal, and landed with a muffled boom just to their right.

Kenny laughed uproariously, and then looked at the house, his eyes growing even wider. 'Is this really ours?'

She nodded, pleased with his reaction. The house was tiny, but exquisite, especially in all the snow. It was an English-cottage style, the tiny window-panes framed from the inside with the big loops of lacy Priscilla curtains. It looked like a haven of warmth and cosiness nestled among the snow, and they went up the path and let themselves in.

'Oh, boy! A fireplace!' Kenny crowed, peeking into the living-room from the entrance hall.

'Take off your boots,' she reminded automatically, looking around. She was pleased anew at how fortunate she had been. The couple that she had rented the house from were going overseas for a year, and had been eager to have someone in who would take good care of their warmly furnished little nest for them.

Charlie and Kenny toured the tiny house from top to bottom.

'I like it,' he announced when the short tour was done.

'Me, too.'

'OK. I think I'll go outside and do something now.' He hopped off his bed, where he had flopped contentedly for a few seconds. He had to duck his head to keep it from hitting the steeply slanting roof, and Charlie felt an unexpected pang of sadness. He looked so tall and handsome, so *normal*, standing there.

She brushed the unwanted thought away. 'I think you'll help me bring in some things from the car, and then we have boxes to unpack.'

'I don't want to,' he said, but without much conviction.

'Tough,' she replied.

He grinned endearingly at her, and she felt guilty for having wished a moment ago that he was any different.

It took them several days to get settled and feeling at home. Charlie was aware of the excitement mounting in her as her first day of work drew closer. The excitement, she was sure, was because she really and truly loved her work. And she loved new experiences, and new challenges. And yet it was none of those things that caused her stomach to flutter with the sensation of a thousand butterflies taking off. Oddly enough, it was the stray thought of brooding sapphire eyes that did that. And probably only because she wondered if Gallagher would be watching her like a hawk, eager to validate his low opinion of professional women by catching her in a mistake. Well, that would only add to the challenge.

Besides, she didn't make mistakes. There was very little margin for error when you flew a helicopter for a living.

CHAPTER THREE

GALLAGHER COLE impaled Charlie with a glance, and put his hand over the telephone receiver. 'You're late,' he bit out, then turned that broad back to her and continued his conversation, his tone to the other party annoyingly civil.

Charlie felt a quiver of anger, which she squelched. His arrogance was slightly justified. She *was* late. Kenny had decided to be difficult this morning. The new housekeeper, a gypsy of a young woman named Tanya, had won Kenny's confidence—and lost Charlie's—by reading Charlie's palm and assuring Kenny that there was no crashed helicopter on the horizon. Charlie had debated all the way to work—a long trip, since she was stuck behind a snow-plough—whether the hocus-pocus was harmless, or whether Kenny, who latched on to goofy ideas rather readily, would be unduly influenced by it.

And she admitted reluctantly that, for some reason, she had expected a bit of a 'welcome aboard' greeting from Gallagher. She had been unprepared for downright rudeness. She wasn't *that* late.

She studied his back momentarily, and found

the study disconcerting. He was a supremely made man, for all his character defects. Which, she reminded herself sternly, would far outnumber even his considerable physical assets. She turned abruptly and feigned rapt interest in the weather chart on the wall behind her.

'Well?'

She had forgotten his voice and the gravelled sensuality of it. When she swivelled slowly and looked at him, she realised that she'd forgotten *him*. Forgotten the intimidating coolness of his eyes, the intimidating strength of his stature.

'I apologise for being late. I wasn't expecting the roads to be in such horrendous condition.' She gave herself a little mental pat for the friendly professionalism of her tone.

'Well, from now on you can expect it,' he retorted coldly. 'You should have been expecting snow. Probably fiddling with your face or some damn thing.'

Her attitude of friendly professionalism deserted her. She stared at him, appalled. She had also managed to forget his utter arrogance in a few short weeks!

'I was not "fiddling with my face",' she returned with thinly veiled fury. 'I do not "fiddle with my face". I apologised for being late, and that's all I can do. It won't happen again.' She knew she should stop there, but her temper had grabbed the reins. 'What's more, I severely doubt that you would ever accuse a male pilot of being late because he was "fiddling with his face".'

'In my experience, men don't have quite the same cavalier attitude towards time that women have,' he shot back, not the least apology in those glittering eyes.

'A cavalier attitude towards time?' she gasped. 'I happened to get caught behind a snow-plough. What does a man do in those circumstances? Hop into the nearest phone booth to change into his Superman outfit so he can fly to work? Besides, you can't tell me that a male member of your staff has never been late.'

'Of course I can't,' he replied. 'Look,' his voice was impatient, 'I'm not an easy man to deal with at this time of year. I've got all kinds of last-minute details to work out. I don't have the time or the inclination to pander to your feminine sensitivities. Just let it slide off your back, OK?'

'Fine,' she managed to croak. It was hardly an apology, after all. Fiddling with her face? Feminine sensitivities? Well, thank heaven that Gallagher Cole was a sexist boor! She was *glad* he was a chauvinist brute—it would make it ridiculously easy to keep her life in its appropriate compartments.

Gallagher was looking at his watch. 'Something's come up. I have to run. The crew is meeting at the One-Twelve at noon for lunch. Be there.'

She stared at him with utter disbelief, then reacted to his tyrannical tone. 'Let me get this straight. You're annoyed with me for being late for work, and we aren't going to work? You're insufferable.' Too late she realised that her temper was really overcoming her good judgement, and that her tone wasn't one a new employee should practise on the boss.

'So quit,' he challenged silkily.

Her anger died as suddenly as it had risen. She regarded him thoughtfully and sombrely. 'You'd like that, wouldn't you?' she guessed. 'It would validate all those second thoughts you've had about hiring a woman if I were to quit in a fit of pique at the first sign of your ugly temper. Plus, then you could guiltlessly do what you wanted to do in the first place—hire a man. Well, I'm not quitting before I've started. If you don't want me here, you should have the guts to fire me. Right now.'

He stared at her incredulously. '*My* ugly temper?' he finally sputtered. 'It seems to me that you have your fair share of temper.'

'I do,' she admitted, her voice level despite her inner quaking. 'I'm a professional. I won't tolerate being treated like an errant schoolgirl for being a few minutes late. And I won't take kindly to being patronised for what you imagine to be my feminine sensitivities!'

OK, it wasn't a tone one should use on a new boss but, as the saying went, start as you mean to go on. And with a man like Gallagher Cole you laid down the ground rules, or found your working conditions intolerable.

'Now,' her voice did not betray the fact that she was shaking uncontrollably inside, 'do I still have a job?' She met his blazing gaze unflinchingly.

For a moment, he looked quite capable of strangling her. But then he shook his head, with a surprising trace of self-mockery. 'I really shouldn't have made that crack about quitting. I need a pilot.'

'Fine. I need a job.'

He shook his head slowly. 'I don't know about this. We need each other, but I don't like personality conflicts on the job, and you and I do not seem to mesh.' He looked at her thoughtfully. 'I wonder if it's because we're different, or because we're the same?'

'Different!' she exclaimed forcefully. 'Very different.'

'I'm not so sure. I have the uneasy feeling that you might be as pig-headed as I am. I'm not used to that.'

She wasn't sure whether to feel flattered or insulted, and he didn't give her time to make up her mind.

'I've got to run. See you at the One-Twelve. At noon. Sharp.'

She turned abruptly away from him. The man did not know how to be civil, even when he was working at it. Sharp, indeed!

Still, she sat in her car for a moment, trying to regain her composure. She was hardly going to be put up for a civility award herself, after her performance this morning. She didn't know what had got into her. She was generally calm and even-tempered to a fault. What was it about that dratted man that got her back so far up that she'd risked a job she needed and had staked her future on to make a point?

At a soft tap on her window, her head jerked up. Gallagher looked through at her, a formidable expression on his face.

Her heart climbed into her throat. He was going to fire her. And not, she admitted, entirely without cause. Not that she didn't feel that she had the right to be treated with respect, but she knew from experience that you couldn't demand it. You had to earn it, particularly as a woman in a man's world. And it *was* important that people working together felt a certain affinity towards each other.

She wound down her window with dread.

'My truck won't start!' he snapped.

She managed, just barely, to suppress a hoot of laughter. Partly because she was relieved that her imaginary scenarios were not coming true, and partly because justice felt wonderful in a world that was not just. She resisted the temptation to point to the phone booth and suggest he change into Superman togs, but she could not resist a sweet smile.

'Can I give you a lift somewhere? I certainly wouldn't want you to be late for an appointment.'

'Don't rub it in,' he growled, coming around

to the passenger side. He climbed in and slammed the door so hard that she winced.

'Where to?' she asked, straight-faced.

'Actually I have a number of places where I have to be this morning.' He was looking straight ahead, his face expressionless.

She decided it would be too cruel to make him beg. Besides, her animosity towards him had dissolved somewhat.

'I'll drive you around.'

'Thanks,' he said gruffly, and a trifle gratefully—the gratefulness, she suspected, was because she was not making the most of the situation to humble him. She decided to use the opportunity to patch some fences.

'Gallagher, we got off on the wrong foot this morning. I apologise for the part I played in that. I do think it's important that we make an effort to get along. I mean, the fact that we're two pig-headed people doesn't have to be such a bad thing. Imagine how invincible we'd be if we ever found something we agreed on.'

He chuckled, and out of the corner of her eye she could see some of the proud stiffness leave him. 'I have a feeling it might be a long time before you and I found any common ground.'

'On a personal level, I agree. But on a professional level you may have been right in suggesting we're more the same than different. I'm a perfectionist, a stickler for detail, committed to being the best at my job that I can be.'

She could tell that she had struck a chord with him, because he gave her a startled look.

'That's me to a T,' he admitted cautiously.

And caution seemed to be the key word for the rest of the morning. They got along fine, but there was a fine tension present, as if both of them were aware how tenuous the peace was, how easy it would be to say the word or express the view that would re-ignite their enmity towards each other. It wasn't entirely comfortable, but it wasn't open warfare, either. Their relationship was already improving, Charlie thought with wry optimism.

At noon Charlie and Gallagher joined a boisterous group at the One-Twelve, a hotel restaurant and lounge which reflected Revelstoke's character in its décor—from old railway pictures on the walls to giant soapstone carvings of grizzly bears.

Charlie was introduced to Leon, the other pilot, Smitty, the engineer, and Rob, one of the ski guides. The other ski guide was a young woman, peachy-complexioned and impish with her hair done in short brown braids.

Gallagher's hand came to rest on the young woman's shoulder as he introduced her. Charlie was taken aback at the open affection that mellowed his eyes when they rested on that upturned pixie face.

'This is Cherry Hillsborough—soon to be a Mrs Cole.'

Charlie had to fight to keep her mouth from

dropping open. *A* Mrs Cole, as if there were a long string of Mrs Coles? And why did she feel both surprised and disappointed that Gallagher had been married, planned to marry again? Men of his age, and particularly of his ilk, came with histories. The girl was far too young for him, but then she should have realised that he had that typical male penchant for sweet young things, from some of the remarks he had made at her interview.

Charlie slipped into the empty chair beside Cherry, trying to put aside her distressing thoughts and concentrate on what Gallagher was saying.

'He's such a sweetie, isn't he?' Cherry murmured in her ear.

A sweetie? The girl was naïve as well as young. Charlie was aware that she had a whole list of things she thought Gallagher was. Overbearing. Stubborn. Insensitive. Chauvinistic. But *sweet*? Never!

'Charlie, you and Leon will fly together this week. He can introduce you to the area while you're flagging landing sites. Even though I know you're aware of the unique perils of helicopter-skiing, maybe you can learn a thing or two from Leon. He's been with us from the beginning.'

Charlie silently added sarcastic to her growing list.

Gallagher moved on to discuss the intricacies of scheduling. Three groups were often booked.

They would be sorted out according to ability, then one group would be dropped, and the helicopter would return for group two. By the time group three was deposited at their first run, group one should be ready to be picked up for their second. Charlie was glad that the guides would be doing dry runs all week, so that the timing could be worked out.

Her list of Gallagher's traits expanded as he spoke, though she reluctantly had to add a few that were less derogatory. He was dedicated. Enthusiastic. Committed. So much so that she found herself dismissing him at a personal level, and allowing herself to become ignited by his energy at a professional one.

A fire of passion crept into his eyes as he spoke, the velvet timbre of his voice was entrancing. He radiated an intensity and a vitality that made his abrasive pig-headedness easy to dismiss as an outer layer. Beneath that rough exterior was a man who dared to dream, who was deeply involved and committed to his way of life. As he spoke, the last faint traces of his sardonic manner were erased from those rugged features, and Charlie allowed herself to feel hope for her future with High Heaven. She wasn't sure that she could ever really like Gallagher, but at least now she was entirely sure that she could respect him.

'We have to get the technical details down so off pat,' he was saying intently, 'that we're the only ones aware that there is a technical side to this business. In other words, I don't want equipment failures. I don't want beginners in the expert groups. I don't want tedious waits at the bottom of runs. I don't want cold lunch. This week we'll be oiling the machine—imagining every possible foul-up, so we can work on prevention now.'

'Didn't this man play the drill sergeant in one of those old B-movies,' Cherry quipped, obviously not intimidated by her husband-to-be. The group laughed and, surprisingly, so did Gallagher.

'OK, I can be a tough man to work for.' He briefly sought out Charlie's eyes, and moved on. 'But I'll tell you why I'm tough. Because I have a goal. To be the best, and to give the best heli-skiing experience in the world.

'What you have to remember is that what we're really doing is running a summer camp for kids—only it's not summer and we're dealing with adults.'

'Exactly like summer camp for kids,' Leon offered, and the high-spirited group laughed again. Charlie felt herself beginning to feel at home with these people, beginning to really look forward to working with them.

Gallagher leaned forward, his expression deadly serious. He dragged a hand through his heavy curls. 'High Heaven succeeds, even though it's small and independent, by providing exactly that essence—the spirit of camp.' Once again his eyes sought Charlie's. 'Did you ever go to camp?'

'Yes,' she said with a smile.

'That's it!' he exclaimed with soft triumph. 'That smile you just smiled is exactly what we're working towards. It was full of fond memories, and just a trace of wistfulness. For what? For days that were endless and perfect and laughter-filled. For camaraderie and a feeling of family, for that sensation of being bonded to nature and the earth. For days that began with exhilaration, and ended with a pleasant kind of exhaustion.

'I've been accused of pandering to a spoiled people,' he continued, a certain ferocious spark in his eyes. 'I've been accused of spending my life glorifying the pursuit of hedonism. But I don't believe that. What I believe is that, if we do our jobs right, we're dealing in the most special of commodities. Joy. It doesn't matter if it's a one-day trip, or a three- or four-day excursion. I want people to leave the High Heaven experience feeling revitalised, hopeful, in touch again with some lost part of themselves, in touch with the world they inhabit.'

Charlie stared at Gallagher incredulously. This couldn't be the same man who had bickered about a few minutes of tardiness this morning. How many sides did he have? And how many of them were this likeable, this admirable? She was aware that he held the group in the palm of his hand. They were totally surrounded by his spell, sitting on the edge of their chairs to catch his next words.

Suddenly she wondered why he was doing this. Why had he tied up a million dollars or more in a helicopter when, with that kind of money and his charisma, his ability to persuade, he could be doing anything? Personal feelings aside, she knew that she was seeing the kind of dynamic and powerful man who could change the world if he set his mind to it.

'People come here to ski. They come for what is probably the best skiing in the world, and they pay big money for the experience. So our greatest challenge is when the weather turns sour. We have to work against intense disappointment, even anger. But that's where we really become a team. Everybody does their part. Nobody is just a guide or just a pilot. You'll be out at my place harnessing horses for sleigh-rides, building snowmen, cross-country skiing. We'll give them memories that will take some of the sting out of not receiving hundred-and-fifty-thousand-feet pins.

'The social side of this experience is every bit as important as the physical side. Remember that. Be prepared to get involved. We don't give people a chance to go back to their rooms and brood about the problems they've left behind. At night we have spectacular dinners, either here or at a special little place called Snuggles. We go to nightclubs, or out to my place to roast marshmallows over an open fire, use the hot-tub, go for sleigh-rides under the moon.

'It really adds something for the clients if they

feel that the staff like them, and enjoy spending time with them. I expect everybody to get involved in our social activities.'

Charlie felt her enthusiasm leave her with a dismal hiss, like the air rushing from a balloon. She wanted to. She wanted to play an integral part in every aspect of this magic spell Gallagher Cole was weaving. But she knew she had to draw lines. She couldn't be away all day for two weeks, and then all night, too. She didn't have the option of calling up a teenage girl to baby-sit every now and then. And Kenny was demanding of her time. He resented her leaving him in the mornings. How would he feel if she started deserting him every night as well? She owed him more than that.

She felt left behind and left out as she watched Gallagher expound on the social events he had planned. She would have to tell him, but how much? People rarely understood Kenny's special problems, and Charlie had developed defences against their insensitivity. Their staring, their snickering, their kind remarks that had a cruel twist, their unintentional condescension.

She felt a need to protect Kenny from the reactions that he was sometimes never even aware of. Protect him, and protect herself.

'And that's the pep talk,' Gallagher concluded. 'Questions?' His eyes found hers as the group was breaking up. 'Stay a minute.'

'Well, what do you think?' he asked when they were alone. He lifted a mug of beer, watched her over its frosty rim. 'It's slightly more than you bargained for, isn't it?'

She could only nod, not the least surprised at how those sharp eyes had been subtly monitoring reactions, and had picked up her distress.

She took a breath and plunged. 'Gallagher, the flying sounds great, and I'm eager to get going. But I can't commit myself to the social side.' She saw a quick flash in his eyes. Disappointment in her. But also relief.

Did he really dislike her that much? She wondered bleakly if maybe she hadn't made a mistake. Coerced him into hiring her on a principle, when personality was going to have so much to do with this job. She hesitated. 'You can start looking for someone else, if the social side is that essential to what you're trying to do.'

She held her breath, afraid that she had acted on pure impulse—made an offer she did not want to have to live up to. It had been different this morning, before she had become fired by his enthusiasm. Now she cared. Still, after this morning there was a good possibility that he was shopping around for her replacement, anyway. They might as well get it out in the open.

His eyes searched her face. 'I thought we'd resolved this this morning. I need a pilot. You need a job. I was aware you had other responsibilities when I hired you. And I hired you anyway. My primary need is for a good pilot, not for a social convener, and not for somebody who kowtows to my every wish, as pleasant as I might find that.

'Still, I think it's obvious that I have some reservations. But I can't very well ask you to commit yourself to my company unless I'm prepared to commit myself to you. So why don't we give it until the end of December? We'll reevaluate the situation then. Until then, consider yourself in. As a pilot. The others can do the social side. I don't really need you for that.'

The last line was spoken quite vehemently, and again Charlie got the impression he was relieved that she wouldn't be playing too large a role in his organisation.

'Anyway, I asked you to stay behind because I wanted to talk to you about pressure. Not because you're a woman,' he stated sarcastically when her mouth opened in automatic protest, 'but because this business has some unique pressures that don't have a thing to do with flying.'

Charlie allowed her mouth to snap closed.

'I probably don't have to tell you that, when it comes to the weather, your word is final. You'll get no argument from me, no matter how many clients are howling their disgust. But it might help you to deal with them if you know how our clients break down.

'They come from all over the world. About twenty per cent Canadian, thirty to forty per cent American, the rest European, with a smattering of Japanese. With the exception of the Japanese, they divide pretty neatly into three groups. We get the very wealthy old-rich. They're basically half-day skiers, who aren't out to prove anything. They come strictly for enjoyment. They like to be treated well, but they also treat others well. They won't be a problem to you, or anybody else.

'On the other end of the scale we have the "ski-nuts". These people are barely better than poverty-stricken. This is a once in a lifetime experience for them. They've saved their money for a long time for it. They're good skiers, dedicated to the sport, and they're easy to please as long as you make every minute count.

'And right in the middle is another group. They can be downright dangerous. The *nouveau riche*. They're in it for the thrill. They talk a better show than they ski. They show off. They're rude and demanding. Nothing is ever good enough and nothing is ever right.'

'I'm not much of a diplomat,' Charlie interceded.

'I think I might have seen that first hand,' he commented drily, 'and actually, at some level, I'm sure it's part of the reason I overcame my reservations and hired you.' He shook his head slightly, as if to say, And look what I've let myself in for.

'Part of the reason you hired me is because we go off like flint against rock?' Charlie asked with disbelief.

Gallagher laughed, and she was uneasily

aware of how she enjoyed the sound of it, the sight of it. It was a robust laugh, that put the sun to shame, that erased a vague world-weariness from his features, that made him seem dangerously warm and approachable.

'I wouldn't say that, exactly. You have a certain stern, no-nonsense attitude I admire—as much as I don't expect it in a woman. When I push, you push back. Now, I may not like it personally, but that's exactly what some of our clients need. Expect to be pushed. And be prepared to push back.'

Stern? No-nonsense? Hardly appealing, Charlie thought, unconsciously giving her head a shake that made her hair cascade around her face, and made her feel slightly less like a pinch-faced, old-maid librarian.

'Maybe strong is the word I'm looking for,' he said absently, and Charlie felt slightly vindicated that he had to pull his straying gaze from her hair.

'The point being?' she asked, a little tersely. She knew that she came on stronger than most women. It was from living out her professional life in a predominantly male world. But she wasn't sure that she wanted to appear strong. The way he had said it, it had conjured up visions of fat, sweating men, grunting mightily under the weight of thousand-pound barbells.

'The point being that skiers can be a difficult bunch to deal with. You have to let them know from second one that you won't stand for any nonsense. They have to know that, as far as that helicopter goes, you're the boss. And you'll have to stay on them. All day, every day. I just wanted you to know I'll be standing behind you. Even on those days—and there will be plenty of them—when you're the last in line for the popularity contest.'

'I appreciate that,' she said with surprised sincerity, and then couldn't resist adding, deadpan, 'And don't worry. My feminine sensitivities won't be in the least offended if I don't win the popularity contest.'

'Good girl,' he said, and saw her wince. 'Your feminine sensitivities are showing,' he remarked.

'I am not a girl,' she stated firmly, 'any more than you are a boy.'

He regarded her thoughtfully. 'You really are a new breed of woman, aren't you? I think that'll be OK as long as you're flying a helicopter. I don't think it's a quality I'd like if you were warming my bed, though.'

The uneasy peace between them was shattered. 'That,' she managed to hiss, 'is an event that is about as likely as pigs being invited to dinner with the Queen——'

'Darn right,' he muttered.

'And what's more,' she continued as if he hadn't interrupted, 'you are exactly the kind of man I despise in my personal life. You lower everything between a man and a woman to its lowest and most base level. You see women as objects—whose only useful purpose on this earth is to warm your bed. Well——'

His eyes were glittering with infuriating amusement. 'I kind of like making you mad,' he admitted softly.

Charlie realised that he had made the remark deliberately, to goad her. She was intensely sorry that she had risen to the bait, but she was also willing to bet that it didn't hide his real attitude by much.

She eyed him narrowly, then changed the subject. 'Why do you do this, anyway? Why would anybody with a million dollars invest in a helicopter? And a lot of hard work? The interest on that money alone could keep you well-heeled for life.'

'But what kind of life?' he returned quietly. 'A life of sitting-by-the-pool-sipping-Scotch leisure wouldn't suit me very well.'

'No, it wouldn't,' Charlie admitted. 'But I know what it costs to maintain a helicopter. Add to that four employees. I also know that, despite a very dear cost to the skier, heli-skiing isn't an enormous money-maker.'

'Worried about your job security?' he asked pointedly.

She shrugged. Let him take it that way if he wanted. In fact, the more time she spent with this man, the more he became a complete enigma. She found herself liking him one minute, questioning her sanity for that liking in the next. What made him tick? If she knew, she could parry his thrusts more effectively.

'We're solvent. I make a decent living. I guarantee your job . . . until December. As for making big money—well, I've done that. It's not what it's cracked up to be.'

The mystery grew again. She reluctantly admired the fact that he had other motivations in life besides money. Maybe, she conceded, watching him, he changed the world after all. In his own way.

'Besides, I never had a million dollars. The helicopter was left to me.' A brief flash of agony passed through his eyes, then was gone. Again, it answered nothing about him, only intensified the mystery.

'Someone left you a helicopter?' she pressed, puzzled.

'A helicopter. A dream.' He stood up, his eyes far away, his words so soft, and so odd, that she could not be sure that she heard him correctly.

'There is more than one way to beat death.'

CHAPTER FOUR

OVER the next week, Gallagher proved to be a hard and relentless taskmaster. He accepted nothing less than perfection from any of them. And yet, despite that, there was a spirit of fun about the group, an excited air of anticipation, as they worked towards becoming the well-oiled team that would be able to present themselves to their clients as calm, professional and competent. Charlie liked the job immensely. And, with everyone working towards a common goal, that animosity that she and Gallagher seemed to spark off each other had disappeared—or been buried for the sake of group unity.

And Charlie's respect for Gallagher grew. His demands and his high expectations pulled them together and brought out the best in all of them. He was a born leader, if a trifle high-handed, and Charlie noted that he inspired something that approached dogged devotion from the people who worked for him. She had also noticed that he worked ten times as hard as any of them. When they were all going home at night, exhausted, the light in his office was still burning. Yes, he was *earning* her respect.

Professionally, anyway.

Charlie waited now, in the helicopter, at the bottom of a hill where two separate runs joined. Rob and Cherry were checking out one, and Gallagher the other. She expected it would be at least ten minutes before she saw either party, and so she was stunned when Gallagher broke over the rise high above her.

She had seen him ski many times in the last week. She knew he was good. No, not just good—superb. A symphony of muscle and motion, in perfect harmony with the mountain. But his power, when he ski'd with others, was leashed. It was only when he ski'd alone, like now, that she saw him unleash that awesome power. It was a sight that never failed to make her heart hammer in her throat. He ski'd the razor's edge, pushing the limits of human capability.

She watched, wide-eyed, as he hurtled down the mountain, hell for leather, crouched, doing nothing to check his speed. The snow boiled up in clouds behind the cutting edge of his skis. The wind grabbed his toque from his head, and tossed it away. For a split second his dark curls sprang free, and then were flattened against his skull.

'He's never going to be able to stop,' she murmured, and shut her eyes. A second later, the eerie silence forced her to open them.

He had stopped, and was now turning, looking back at the slope in silent salute, his broad shoulders heaving. He slipped from his skis, threw them effortlessly over his shoulder, and ambled over to the helicopter.

She felt an inexplicable anger with him, and glared at him when he hopped into the helicopter.

'Is that what you meant by ''there's more than one way to beat death''?' she snapped, aware suddenly that the phrase had bothered her all week.

He looked at her with faint surprise, ran his fingers through thick hair that sparkled with tiny diamonds of ice and sweat.

'No. What made you think so?'

Her voice was strained. 'Because that's how you act out there when you're on your own. Reckless. Devil-may-care. As if you're challenging death, and winning . . . for now.'

'Do I?' he asked mildly. His blue eyes settled on her with faint mockery, asking why she cared.

'I don't have a lot of respect for people who will risk everything for a thrill,' she informed him coldly. She told herself that she did not care how he ski'd at all. She just didn't want to be the one left to pick up the mutilated wreckage of that magnificent body when he pressed too far and ended up smeared all over a rock-face. That was what made her angry, and that was all.

Well, maybe there was a bit more involved. He was a very vital man to be around when he ski'd. He exuded energy, and power; he exuded that mysterious force that was life itself. And that force washed over her, and in those moments she cared about him. Not as a woman to a man. Not on a romantic or sexual level. Oh, hell, she thought, there were just times, as few and far between as they might be, when he stopped being arrogant and obnoxious for long enough that he was a little bit likeable. So what?

Out of the corner of her eye, she caught sight of Cherry and Rob making their way down the second run. She turned her attention to the red-clad figure bobbing gracefully down the slope. She liked Cherry. She had been surprised to learn that the younger woman was twenty-two. She looked sixteen and, in Charlie's mind, acted it, too. Irrepressible, high-spirited, bubbly. Nice, but not the woman for Gallagher. He needed something different. Maturity. Depth. Strength. He needed someone who wouldn't be completely overpowered by his arrogance. Someone who wouldn't be afraid to keep him in line. And she heartily pitied anyone foolish enough to take on that task—particularly Cherry, since she seemed so ill-equipped for the job.

She slanted Gallagher a look to see if he was watching Cherry. He was, but his face was impassive. Charlie was fascinated by their interactions—or rather, their lack of them. Their relationship struck her as being oddly without sizzle, like that of an older brother and a younger sister. If Gallagher felt any passion for the younger woman, he masked it well behind his professionalism. Could a man like Gallagher mask passion? She doubted it.

'It's not just a thrill,' he said suddenly.

'No?' Charlie arched an eyebrow at him. 'I can't think of a more dangerous sport. It encompasses too many variables—weather conditions, snow-packs, human and technical limitations. A lot of our best runs are located in avalanche chutes, for pete's sake. I think, in the end, sometimes these mountains can't be tamed. People get hurt. People die. And for what, if not that thrill of looking death in the face?'

'From the lady who flies helicopters for a living,' Gallagher said drily.

'A helicopter's a machine. It runs by precise and predictable rules. I'm the one who controls the machine and, if I do my job right, chances of things going wrong are very slim. You can't tell me a mountain is like that.'

'You'll have to ski it with me one day.' It sounded more like an order than an invitation. But then, practically everything he said sounded that way. Then his tone softened, as it unexpectedly did sometimes. 'I want you to feel it so you'll know it's so much more than a thrill. It's being more fully alive than a man can ever hope to be. It's being entirely sensitised to your environment, to how you fit into the universe, to your capabilities, to the strength of the mountain. Worth dying for? I guess it is, because in some way the mountain allows a glimpse of what life is all about. I think people are a little more accepting of the concept of death if they've felt the full glory of life.

'It's true that death might be waiting in the next moment, but it's hard to care when you're totally engrossed in this moment. I like the way the Indians used to put it. They used to say "it's a good day to die". But not on a rotten day when they felt down, no, only on the best of days, when it felt so incredibly good to be alive.'

'I wonder how a philosophy like that holds up to reality?' Charlie asked, her dubious note intentional. She did not want Gallagher to know that he was capable of moving her on rare occasions. He would see that as feminine and weak, and probably start a campaign to get himself a bed-warmer . . . or get rid of her. 'I'm sure you'd feel differently if it were a close friend buried under sixteen tons of snow.'

'It was,' he said quietly, unconsciously stroking the jagged scar on his face. 'It was.'

'You were in it, too, weren't you?' she asked softly. 'An avalanche?'

'Yes.'

In that moment, she knew she would try the deep-powder experience, when he asked her. He had paid so much, and still found it worth the price. She suddenly *had* to know what was up here that could inspire such courage . . . or such bull-headed stupidity.

'White-out.' Charlie's voice sounded calm. She realised that she felt calm. Detached. In control.

It just went to show that you never really knew—even yourself. She had thought she would feel blind terror if she ever encountered this most dreaded of flying conditions.

'Would you wipe that look off your face?' Gallagher's voice crackled through her headphone.

She spared him the briefest of glances. He was obviously feeling enough terror for both of them.

'What look?' Her eyes were narrow, scanning for the ground, for the briefest break in the sudden weather that had wrapped itself around them like a white blanket.

'That look of grim fatalism. Hell, I can tell by the set of your mouth, we're in trouble.'

'We are. Watch for the ground.'

'Which direction might that be?' he asked sarcastically.

'You won't be able to see it with your eyes closed.'

'Shut up, and drive.'

She saw it then. Thought she did. A brief break in the swirling snow, just enough that she could make out a faint line of dimension that she hoped was land. She took a chance. Lightly, lightly, lightly. Praying that she wasn't already so disorientated that she might be going sideways instead of down.

A comforting thud. They were down. On solid, level ground. She closed her eyes, let her head loll forward, and rubbed the knotted muscles in her neck.

'Thank heaven,' Gallagher murmured tersely.

'Unless we're sitting on an ice-shelf or the edge of a cliff.'

'Did you have to say that?'

She glanced at him. His face was white, strained.

'It's like being dropped into the centre of a milk bottle and given a good shake, isn't it?'

'Exactly like that,' he agreed, his voice totally lacking its normal confidence.

Charlie looked out. It was still exactly like that. Walls of impenetrable white all around them. Reaction began to set in. She closed her eyes again, the consequences of one false move playing out in her mind, now that none of them had happened. She began to shake.

'You did magnificently,' Gallagher said, his tone gentle for once. Strong hands took up the massage of her neck.

She didn't want him touching her. It would be too easy to creep into his arms like a frightened child and weep. But his hands felt so good, she couldn't stop him.

Instead, she tried to construct a barrier of words. 'Gallagher, if you still want to fire me, now you have reason.' She had meant to sound calm. Her voice quivered.

'Are you kidding? We're alive! Consider yourself signed on for life.'

She smiled feebly. 'I made a mistake, Gallagher. I shouldn't have suggested hopping.' It was their final day of preparation before skiers arrived. The cloud had come in, but she had decided that she and Gallagher could safely 'hop', fly below the cloud following sheltered ravines and valleys, to get a feel for both the flying conditions and the skiing beneath the cloud. Then, in one of the valleys, the weather had thickened with impossible swiftness, accompanied by a swirling wind.

'Charlie, I know you're good, but you couldn't have predicted this. Nobody could have. So forget it.'

She smiled gratefully. 'OK, but you had your chance.' She knitted her brow, looking out into the white again. 'I wonder how long we're going to be here?'

'Who cares? We're alive.'

She laughed. 'You're remarkably amicable when you've had a close call. I'll have to remember that.'

'Are you threatening me with a scare every time I get a little nasty? I'm going to have enough trouble getting back into one of these contraptions, without having to wonder about that.'

'Gallagher, after seeing you ski, I really believed you were a man without fear. But you were really terrified. What happened to "it's a good day to die"?'

'Today isn't,' he said emphatically. 'Besides, when I ski, I'm so focused on life. A few minutes ago, I was focused on death. Didn't you think we were going to die?'

'I didn't think about it while we were up,' she said honestly. 'I'm thinking about it now that we're down.'

'I hope you appreciate the irony of this. I hesitated to hire you because I thought you might panic under pressure. And who panicked? Certainly not old stone-face James.'

'"Stone-face"?' she echoed grimly.

'It was just your expression.' He took in the wounded look that she was too exhausted to try and hide, and sighed. 'You don't need me to tell you you're a beautiful woman.'

'No, I don't,' she agreed woodenly. Especially not now. She was alone with him in isolation as intense as it got. She was feeling the after-effects of both adrenalin and relief. It would be too easy to give into a purely physical celebration of this moment. To seek the warmth, the strength, the comfort, of his arms, his lips . . . She forced her eyes away from those lips.

She had just seen a vulnerable side to Gallagher. For the first time, probably for the only time. It was compelling. She slid away from the hands that still rested on her neck, suddenly too aware of how they offered not only comfort, but electrical promise . . .

'I think it's lifting.'

'Think? You make bloody well sure. And another thing——'

She was relieved that, with the lifting of the snow, he was returning to his ordinary autocratic self.

'Never mind, Gallagher. I won't breathe a word.'

He glared at her. 'How did you know?'

'A lucky guess,' she said drily.

'Hell, you're cheeky. I might fire you after all.'

He was teasing her. She didn't like it. It made her feel oddly warm. Oddly close to him. Well, things would be back to normal soon enough. Or would they?

Once you had seen the sun streaking through the clouds, did you ever really stop looking for it again?

Charlie watched Gallagher closely the next morning as he gave a polished orientations presentation to their first group of skiers. He seemed none the worse for their little adventure. He seemed as magnetic, as powerful—as fearless—as ever.

'OK?' she asked in a low voice into her headset when they were finally ready to go, and he was settled beside her.

He gave her a disparaging look. 'Any reason I wouldn't be?'

'It would be entirely human to be a little nervous.'

'Are you?'

'No.'

'Then I'm not, either.' There was a long silence. 'But if I were,' his voice crackled softly in her ear, 'you can bet your bottom dollar that I wouldn't let it show in front of the clients.

They'd probably start bailing out.'

'In that case, don't you so much as sweat, Gallagher Cole!'

Their eyes met for a moment. Charlie looked for the sunshine, found it. They shared something now. A strange intimacy came out of the power of a crisis experience. She sensed that he had tried to break that bond, to deny it, and couldn't. But she also sensed that he would try again.

It was an exciting day. The high spirits of the skiers were remarkably contagious. Their faces, as they reboarded the helicopter after each run, were beautiful to see. Their eyes held a quality very close to ecstasy. Charlie knew they had just enjoyed one of the most unique experiences in the world, as different as night from day from what they would encounter on commercial ski-slopes that were groomed and peppered with people, and had short runs interspersed with long queues at the chair-lifts. Being around these people reinforced Charlie's decision to try skiing the high powder at the first opportunity. That decision had nothing to do with an appetite that had been whetted to share more experiences with Gallagher Cole!

Finally, all three groups were back at the airport, chattering excitedly, reluctant to say goodbye to the experience by boarding the buses. This despite the cold and their obvious weariness.

'Opening night is usually pretty special,'

Gallagher said non-committally. 'Why don't you try and join us for this one?'

'I can't tonight,' she said, and he turned from her abruptly. She wondered at his abruptness. Had their experience in the white-out left him with the beginnings of a frightening thirst, too? A thirst to share more experiences? Did he feel he had allowed himself to be vulnerable, and been rejected for his efforts? She was sorry if he was feeling those things, but she had other responsibilities, and she couldn't just duck out on them at a moment's notice.

'Maybe tomorrow?' This was from a young man who had been listening—and ogling her all day—and his voice was eager.

'Probably not tomorrow, either.' She caught a glimpse of Gallagher's profile. Did he look so thunderous because of the young man's interest, or because of her own lack of involvement in the social side, even though he had said once that he understood?

No, she decided firmly, he looked that way because that was what he was—a thunderous tyrant, and she would do well not to forget it.

Still, she felt disappointed. Though she hadn't been skiing, she had shared much of the exhilaration of the day, and she knew that she was unquestioningly accepted as part of the group.

'Gallagher,' she said, touching his arm, 'I'll talk to my sitter. Maybe she'll agree to come in one night a week as well.'

'Don't put yourself out,' he said indifferently.

There, she thought, it was over. The tenuous bond between them had lasted less than twenty-four hours. Too bad. It might have helped them work together more harmoniously. Then again, all day long she'd been finding the firm line of his lips distracting, so maybe it wouldn't have at all.

'Fine,' she said coolly, 'I won't put myself out.'

He shrugged, and for a reason she couldn't fathom she felt an uncharacteristic desire to hit him. Instead, she turned on her heel, her spine straight, and walked away.

'You're in a bad mood,' Kenny announced to her over dinner.

His observation startled her. She was trying very hard to be in a good mood. The fact that it wasn't working was unsettling. Was there a possibility that she had more invested in what Gallagher thought of her than she was prepared to admit? Thankfully, Kenny did not give her time to dwell on it.

'I'm in a good mood. I met Tanya's brother today. He's neat, Chuck. We're going to be friends.'

Charlie was regaled with tales of Mike for the remainder of their meal. It became apparent that he shared Kenny's handicap, but still had a job. Mike had a girlfriend. Mike was going to get his own apartment soon. Charlie felt her head beginning to ache. Because, in each recounting of what Mike did, despite the bubbling voice, she sensed something like reproach in Kenny's eyes, something that asked, How come I'm not doing everything Mike's doing?

And she didn't know why, and was reluctant to think about it. But, unwillingly, she remembered that at the special school Kenny had attended they had attempted to prepare Kenny for some kind of semi-independence. He had been taught a life-skills programme. He had some very rudimentary reading skills. He could find the men's toilet, and read 'Walk' and 'Don't Walk' signs. He had a cookbook that used pictures instead of words. He had learned how to work a washer and dryer. But, since he had finished school, she knew she was guilty of letting it all backslide. She did everything for him, generally because it was easier that way. And after one disastrous work experience, she'd decided never to put him through something like that again.

She wondered why she suddenly felt guilty. Kenny's life was uncomplicated and problem-free. She protected him, she nurtured him. For heaven's sake, her whole life revolved around doing the best for him. She felt a vague and familiar uneasiness pressing the edges of her mind. She dismissed it sharply, realising how tired she was. She went to bed.

Charlie worked fourteen days straight and, for

the most part, enjoyed her job immensely. It was totally engrossing, and it was challenging. She liked the staff, and she liked the clients, despite the fact that Gallagher had been entirely correct in telling her that she would have to keep an eye on them all day, every day.

Gallagher continued to be a problem. His attitude towards her was baffling. Annoying. Irritating. He treated her with a rather chilly professionalism. Nothing more. Nothing less. It had seemed for a short time, trapped on a snowbound mountain, that they might be able to see beyond their dislike of each other's views. But, if anything, that moment of vulnerability had made the wall go up higher, not provided the crack that would weaken it until it fell.

His attitude shouldn't have irked her at all, she realised. She should have no investment in how Gallagher Cole chose to behave. And it was not as if he ever broke the bounds of propriety. It was not as if he was rude or snarling. It was just that his indifference was so exclusive to her. With everyone else he was on excellent terms. With the crew and the clients she saw him being encouraging. Charming. Courteous. Occasionally authoritative. And even occasionally playful. All were roles he stepped into with the equal ease of one totally at home with himself. With the masterful confidence of one who did not wear masks—and yet always, it seemed, his face wore a smooth mask when he dealt with her.

Still, she refused to try and break through that mask. She did not suggest getting a sitter again. She didn't do it because the very fact that she did find him so intriguing posed a vague danger. He was the sort of man whom you could find you were in over your head with—before you were even aware that you had entered the water!

And already, despite the fact that she knew Cherry would be his wife some day, despite the fact that he could be aggravating and irritating, she knew an outlaw part of herself *liked* being around him. She liked watching the way he interacted with others, interacted with rugged rock and snow. She was drawn to the energy and passion that burned in him like an inner light—a light she was sure had lured more than one on to the rocky shores of his intrigue.

Her first two weeks of work ended. For all of the last week, she was aware of waiting to see if he would ask her skiing on one of her days off. He didn't mention it and, given his attitude, she should have been neither surprised nor hurt. In fact, she was both.

Her two weeks off dragged. Revelstoke did not provide the same array of activities as the big city had, and it was more difficult to keep Kenny busy and entertained all day. He began to nag her about taking him up in the helicopter. If her relationship with Gallagher had been running more smoothly, she might have capitulated to the pressure. As it was, she doubted she would ever broach the subject of Kenny with

Gallagher. Kenny was her soft underbelly, and somewhere along the way, she knew not where, she had given Gallagher the power to wound her. His opinion mattered to her. And over the two weeks off she found that her mind drifted to him, relived certain moments, certain words, the midnight-blue of those unfathomable eyes, the flash of white teeth against bronzed skin.

Yes, her mind drifted to him in absolute and unconcerned defiance of the iron will she had always been able to exercise over restless thoughts and feelings. Why did it keep insisting on dredging up the deep blue of his steady gaze?

Besides, he was committed to Cherry. Besides, never had two people with such different views and philosophies been forced to spend so much time together. Perhaps it was only her growing respect for him that had triggered this illogical fantasy that she would like to know him better. Perhaps it was even less. Perhaps it was just that age-old need of wanting to be liked, approved of, even by those you didn't particularly like or approve of yourself.

Charlie rose, on the morning she was to return to work, to find snow such as she had never seen falling in huge, heavy flakes outside her window. It was not weather for helicopters. She felt an acute ache of disappointment within her. It started like a ping-pong ball in the pit of her stomach. By the time she'd finished her first cup of coffee, the disappointment was beach-ball sized.

Then the phone rang.

'I've got twenty-nine Japanese tourists to look after. Know anything about horses?' There was no need for the caller to identify himself.

'Horses?' she echoed stupidly.

'Never mind. I'll be by to get you in half an hour.'

She'd been talking to him for thirty seconds, and already she felt her antagonism towards him rising—which made her mental meandering of the past fourteen days even more baffling. But couldn't the man ever ask? Did he always have to come across as so commanding and controlling?

'I'll drive myself, thanks,' she said stiffly.

His silence sizzled, and she had the uncomfortable feeling that he was thinking the exact thought she had just had.

'Have you looked out of your window?'

'Yes,' she said stubbornly. If he could drive on a day like this, so could she.

'Have you, perchance, looked at your car?' His tone dripped with pseudo-patience.

'No, but——'

'Fine. Go and look at your car, Lady Rambo. I'll be there in half an hour.'

The phone clicked in her ear before she got a chance to say something extremely rude. If she was fighting mad when she hung up, she was even madder as she scrambled over the six-foot mountain of snow that had been ploughed into her driveway exit, and slid down the other side to Gallagher's waiting truck.

'Would you look at that?' she fumed, climbing into the truck and slamming the door.

'Good morning to you, too,' Gallagher interjected drily.

She ignored him. 'Can you believe the nerve? They must have seen my car there, and they ploughed me in anyway. Somebody from the town hall is going to be getting an earful from me! I——'

'I'm sure they took one look at your car, decided it belonged to a woman, and figured you wouldn't be going anywhere. That you'd be sitting around all day sipping tea——'

'How dare you imply I have a chip on my shoulder?' She turned her fury quite readily on him.

'I was teasing. For heaven's sake, would you say the Serenity Prayer, or something? Our clients will take one look at your face, and be so frightened they'll be trying to swim back to the land of the rising sun.'

Despite herself, she burst out laughing. 'Do *you* find me that frightening, Mr Cole?'

He nodded solemnly. 'You're definitely the most frightening woman I've ever met.'

Despite his teasing tone, she sensed a kernel of truth there.

'I wouldn't bother unleashing your temper on the town hall, either. Nothing except four-wheel drives will be moving today. This truck and both

of the buses are equipped. I suspected that your
car was not. Rob and Cherry have taken the
buses and the clients out to my place. You and I
are going to pick up the lunch and meet them
out there.'

The roads were very nearly impassable, and
even with the four-wheel drive they got stuck
three times as they inched their way out of town
toward Gallagher's acreage. It was oddly fun,
though. There was a spirit of adventure about
tackling these roads together. She enjoyed
watching Gallagher pit his sheer determination
against the road conditions, and yet keep his
good humour, as though he were in his element
rising to challenges like these.

Finally, they pulled off the main highway, and
slithered down a steep track to the valley below.
The road wound through thick cedar, and then
suddenly they burst into a gently rolling, snow-
covered meadow. At the top of a small knoll was
a very contemporary log home.

Charlie gasped her appreciation as they pulled
up beside it. 'It's beautiful!'

Gallagher looked at the house, and grinned
with a surprising trace of humility. 'Thanks. I
built it myself.'

She studied the house, and then him.
Somehow the thought of him pouring his sweat
and love into this house altered her view of him.
Which was what? That he was a fast-living, self-
important skirt-chaser, she supposed.

'Sometimes, I don't think you're what you

appear to be,' she commented quietly.

'Are any of us?' he asked, and they stood there, looking deeply at each other, feeling a whisper of appreciation, a tiny breeze that tempted discovery.

'We should put this stuff in the house, get the snow-mobile and catch the others,' he suggested. But he didn't move.

'Yes,' she agreed. But she didn't move either.

'Or,' he said after a long time, 'we could just go into the house.'

The yes whispered through her brain, but never left her lips. She felt confusion well up inside her and heat her cheeks. She didn't know what he was suggesting, but she felt suddenly very cautious. It could well be that he was *exactly* what he always appeared to be, and that would mean he wouldn't be above taking advantage of her softened mood.

'We'd better catch the others,' she said.

He shrugged, his expression unreadable, making his intentions even less clear and her confusion even greater. But she almost wished she'd chosen the house once they were mounted on the snow-mobile and gliding powerfully through a fairy-tale of white.

Because, surely, whatever they could have done or said there wouldn't have been as breathtaking as this wordless ride? Charlie had to wrap her arms tightly around his midsection, and she could feel the movement of his muscle beneath his jacket, the lean hardness of him, the heat of his body. The wind tangled her hair and splashed colour into her cheeks as she looked over the breadth of his shoulder. Again, they were plunged into a shared intimacy, sailing through a snowbound world so glorious that her heart ached from its beauty.

She didn't know if she was relieved or regretful when they arrived at the top of a hill to find a huge, hay-laden sleigh, two giant horses, and twenty-nine Japanese people cavorting with toboggans.

Gallagher went to the horses immediately, and Charlie's confusion about him increased. Who would have guessed that such a gentle side existed in him? The horses were bunting him fondly with giant heads. He talked to them in a low, affectionate tone while he checked their harnesses. He had an apple for each of them in his pockets. Who was this man?

'Good job, Cherry, Rob,' he said approvingly. 'Really good job.'

Gallagher did not give praise lightly, and Rob and Cherry beamed. He turned back to Charlie.

'Well, let's not set a bad example,' he said. 'Get on one of those things, and get going.'

'I was looking for the controls,' she protested, eyeing a toboggan warily.

'No excuses.'

'I will, if you will,' she challenged.

Without another word, Gallagher grabbed her and set her down firmly on a toboggan. He climbed on behind her, and wrapped one steely arm around her waist. He used the other to give the toboggan a push, and then wrapped that one around her as well.

She would have been hard-pressed to tell what brought the roses blooming in her cheeks, her heart hammering at the walls of her chest. Was it the wind in her face? The thrill of the wild ride? Or was it Gallagher's strong arms wrapped so solidly around her, his frosty breath stirring the hair at the back of her neck?

Whatever it was, it felt good. She threw her contemplations of Gallagher's true character, her confusions, her caution, to the wind. Feelings like this were not intended to be analysed. They were meant to be embraced. She grabbed the elusive feeling with both hands, and hugged it to her breast as though she would never have to face the moment when she would have to let it go.

CHAPTER FIVE

GALLAGHER and Charlie shot down the hill on the racing toboggan. She didn't know when she had last laughed so hard, felt so wonderfully carefree. Maybe it was back in those days of summer camp.

Their sled suddenly hit a bump of snow, careened into the shelter of some trees, and flipped. Charlie found herself tumbling through the air. She landed on her back with a painless thump, and Gallagher landed right on top of her. She was choking on snow and laughter. So was he. If joy had a sound, this was it. His deep, unchecked aughter delightfully disturbing the silence of the snowbound forest.

Their eyes locked together, the laughter faded and then died. They were back in a moment she had tried to escape once already today. Perhaps it was inescapable, after all.

As if in a trance, Gallagher's hand moved to her face, tucked a loose tress of hair back under her toque, brushed the snow from her cheeks, and then lingered, his fingers and his eyes conveying a message that made her begin to quake with something quite different from laughter.

She freed her own hand from where it was crushed between them, reached out and traced the

84

lines of his face, not thinking, just instinctively rising to what the moment offered.

For a long moment he let her explore his face, his hungry, half-lidded eyes burning with unbearable sensuality. She became aware of his weight, of the hard wall of his chest crushing her breasts, of those iron-sheathed legs locked around hers. The aroma of a spicy cologne, and another smell—entirely male, and utterly pleasant—wafted into her nostrils.

His eyes were darkening, light flickering in them like the sparks of a fire against the deep midnight-blue of a night sky.

She had seen it coming, had been forewarned by his eyes, but she was still startled when his mouth touched hers. His lips ran, teasing and taunting, over her own. Sparks against a night sky. Sizzling. Exploding upwards. Dying even as the next had already begun.

The kiss intensified, sparks turning to fire, melting to white-hot flame. She, like a moth, driven by instinct into the heart of the flame, though it felt as if it would turn her to ash, this feeling that came from him and yet also leapt, molten, within her.

'Charlie? Gallagher? Are you two all right?' Rob's voice broke in from a long way away, and Charlie heard it but didn't react, unwilling to turn away from the fire, back to the real world of snow and ice.

But Gallagher rolled off her abruptly, lay on his back in the snow, regarding the sky with a scowl, his breathing heavy.

'Fine,' he shouted at Rob, and then got to his feet with lazy, liquid grace.

The scowl was still on his face, and she scrambled to her feet, colour flooding her cheeks. What on earth was she doing? She was not the loose and lusty type—not that you would know it from the way she had just behaved. She had just blithely and blissfully broken her cardinal rule—that she did not *ever* get involved like this with people she worked with.

Good lord. What was he doing? Cherry could have come through those trees in search of him at any time. *A* Mrs Cole, she remembered bitterly. How many Mrs Coles? How many affairs? Don't be like *that*, Gallagher, she pleaded inwardly. But hadn't she always wondered if he was like that? That strong body oozed such easy sensuality. She had watched the women on trips flutter around him like clucking hens. Watched him accept their attentions as if they were his due, watched him make them blush and coo. OK, she had never personally witnessed him step over the line of his professionalism, but then again, she never saw him socially. Was he a different man then? As he was a different man today?

She busied herself brushing the snow from her clothes, the kiss from her lips.

'I don't know what came over me,' she said tightly. Or you, she added to herself.

His scowl deepened. 'I always had my doubts about a man and a woman being able to work together without something like that happening.'

Was there faint accusation in his voice? Did he believe that she had invited that—that attack?

Without warning his scowl faded and his voice softened. 'I don't like complications that affect my business. On the other hand,' his eyes, intensely blue, caught on her lips, 'it would be very tempting to let nature take its course.'

After that heart-stopping kiss, there was no avoiding his meaning. Charlie knew precisely what course nature would take.

'You know, Gallagher,' her tone was stinging, 'I would have thought you loyal, if nothing else. I was wrong.'

He looked puzzled, and then his gaze clouded, and a look of pain danced briefly across his features before he looked away from her.

But he had remembered Cherry too late for her to feel sympathy for him. 'Remembering your fiancée?' she asked with cold cruelty, punishing him for her own multi-faceted disappointment.

He jerked his head back towards her, and she saw that her barb had hit. Too hard. For a moment she shrank back, wondering if, in his fury, he was capable of hitting her. But those powerful fists remained clenched at his sides, and then the anger drained from his eyes. Life itself seemed to drain from his eyes. His gaze was hard and cold and bleakly empty.

Wordlessly he stooped, picked up the toboggan, stuffed it under his arm and strode away. His back was stiff and unyielding. He did not turn to see if she followed him.

The snow-mobile was gone by the time Charlie trudged up the hill. She was still fuming that he had looked at her as if she had wronged him, when he was the one who was the traitor!

Cherry came and sat beside her in the hay, ignoring the signals her hunched shoulders and cold expression should have given.

'What happened in those bushes, anyway?' she asked eagerly.

'Nothing.'

'Come clean! I can read faces. He stole a kiss, and you slugged him, right? You must have hit him pretty hard. He looked like he'd been through the wars when he roared out of here.'

Charlie was appalled. What kind of world was this? How could Cherry be so free and easy about the man she was going to marry?

'If you want an explanation,' her voice squeaked with disgust, 'I suggest you go and ask Gallagher for it. I'm sure it will be the first of many explanations you'll have to ask him for in your married life.' She was instantly regretful of both her words and her tone. But Cherry was not looking insulted. She looked stunned.

'Married life? With Gallagher?' She hooted with unexpected delight. 'Me? Marry Gallagher? For heaven's sake, Charlie, he's *old*!'

'But . . . but, I thought he introduced you as the future Mrs Cole.' Charlie could feel a mortified blush creeping up her cheeks.

Cherry laughed. 'That's me, all right. I think we

all kind of forget you're new to this community where everybody knows everything about everyone. Gallagher's younger brother, Bob, and I have been dating for years. We've decided to get married in the spring.'

Cherry took in Charlie's fire-red cheeks, and clapped with mirth. 'This is wonderful! Oh, I kept hoping something would happen between the two of you. Will it now? Now that,' she giggled, 'the other woman is out of the way?'

'I doubt it,' Charlie said tersely. It occurred to her that the answer should have been an emphatic 'no!'

Cherry grew suddenly serious. 'That's too bad. It's been such a long time for him. He needs something in his life besides his darned business, but he's too stubborn to admit it. Men! Caring hurts them once, and they're determined never to care again.'

'Humph! I find it hard to believe that the invincible Mr Cole was ever that badly hurt. I had him pegged as the "love 'em and leave 'em" type.'

'He is—now. He wasn't always. And he's not as much that way as he'd like the world to believe. I think he works at scaring people away so he never really has to find out if he's over it, if he's strong enough to love again. He thinks he isn't, you know. I think he's wrong.'

'What happened to him?' Charlie asked, curious despite her intense desire not to be.

'His fiancé died. In a skiing accident several

years ago.'

'An avalanche,' Charlie guessed dully, remembering, sickly, that day she'd accused him of holding philosophies that couldn't stand up to reality.

She felt the blood draining from her face. And she had just accused him again—of being disloyal to his fiancé. What must he think of her? What fresh pain had she unwittingly cost him? What fresh distrust of caring would her words have inspired?

Gallagher took charge of the horses when they arrived back and, while the others trooped towards the house, Charlie held back. She slipped into the barn behind him.

'Hi.' He didn't answer, and she studied his profile, resisting an absurd impulse to reach up with her fingertips and touch him, as if a gesture of softness could melt the fierce hardness from those remote features.

'Gallagher, I came to apologise. I thought—have always thought—that you were engaged to Cherry. I'm sorry if I inadvertently opened some old wounds. I'm even more sorry for accusing you of a disloyalty that didn't exist.'

The eyes rested briefly on her face, and then he shrugged and turned back to his horses.

'Forget it.' His voice was controlled, uncaring. Then, just in case she had missed his meaning, he added with soft killing, 'Forget all of it.'

Her mission of mercy was over! *Forget all of it*? As if she had come in here begging for a second kiss!

But her anger died as quickly as it had flared. Because she saw something more than the cool invulnerability he was showing her, saw something more than the cold, hard strength in his face and his stature. She nodded wordlessly, and left the barn.

The house also reflected that 'something more' about Gallagher. He had unconsciously exposed his soul when he had built and decorated this house. Inside was golden wood, coupled with stone, and accented with a jungle of glorious green plants. Light poured in from everywhere—through large windows, and the skylights in the sloping ceiling. Even on this grey day, there was an atmosphere of brightness, of cosiness. A large, soft grey sectional sofa added a dimension of sensuality to the living-room. It was dotted with bright cushions, the colours picked up again in several large prints of native art that adorned the walls. But it was not a bachelor pad—did not even remotely suggest a swinging life-style. It was a haven of tranquillity that radiated solidness, warmth and character.

The day went downhill, and Charlie had never been so glad to see a day over.

The following week continued to be overshadowed with a horrendous tension, though the Japanese were excellent skiers and guests. They were courteous, and followed instructions without reminding, argument or complaint. They were often unintentionally hilarious. When Charlie first introduced them to the helicopter, the interpreter had listened to her solemnly, and then summed up her speech by pointing at the blades, slicing his throat with his hand, and proclaiming an emphatic, 'Chop-ee, chop-ee!'

It had been a sign of the week to come that she hadn't laughed. Her laughter had been left somewhere among the silence of snow-bent trees. She had glanced at Gallagher. He was not laughing either.

One kiss. One broken rule. Never again, she vowed. Never! And she prayed that, when the memory faded for both of them, things would return to normal. Normal? There had yet to be normal for them. What she wanted was so little—an ordinary, friendly, courteous working relationship. But now—now she had seen desire set his eyes on fire. Would normal ever be enough again? Perhaps it was safer, if not exactly comfortable, the way things were.

'Charlie.'

They were done for the day. The well-satisfied Japanese clients would be returning home tomorrow. New groups would be coming in. She had missed the sound of her name on his lips.

'They've asked if they could have one more sleigh-ride. Because both Rob and Cherry are going to be busy tonight, I had just planned a movie. I hate to send them home disappointed, but I can't manage it myself, either.'

His words were stiff, and she knew it had taken a great deal of effort for him to ask her for help. But still, he *had* unbent enough to ask. She saw in that the potential to start again. The potential for 'normal'. Her heart sank.

'I'm sorry, Gallagher, I just can't. Not tonight.'

His eyes cooled. The potential of the moment, of a healing evening of lightness and laughter, was gone.

She longed to tell him. Tell him that she had planned to take Kenny to the movie all week, and each night she had come home feeling so tired and tense, she had begged off. There was only one cinema in Revelstoke, and Kenny had informed her irritably that tonight was the last night for the show he wanted to see. She had promised. Not just said 'maybe', but promised. Kenny knew the difference between a 'we'll see' and a 'promise. So did she. She would have loved to soften the hard, unyielding line of Gallagher's face with an explanation, but it was an explanation that needed time. Trust. Compassion. He was already turning his broad back to her.

She could do nothing more than watch him walk away.

Kenny was in one of his more difficult moods when she got home.

'I want to go and see the movie now,' he demanded for the tenth time as they ate the delicious dinner Tanya and Kenny had prepared together.

'Oh, Kenny! I told you no. It's far too early.'

'I want good seats,' he told her sulkily, and then revealed the true source of his bad temper. 'You got to go on a sleigh-ride this week. You got to be in the helicopter. I didn't get to do nothing. You never do fun things with me.'

Hit where it hurts, Kenny, she thought wearily. Push the old guilt-button. 'We'll have fun tonight,' she soothed.

'Only if we get good seats,' Kenny came back stubbornly.

Kenny's mood did not improve as they walked the few blocks to the cinema. He was belligerent and difficult.

'I'm cold. Why didn't we drive?'

'For heaven's sake, Kenny! You would have been just as cold in the car—colder.'

'I want a big popcorn,' Kenny said in the queue outside the cinema. 'And some liquorice. And a large Coke. Two Cokes——'

'A popcorn, and one small pop,' she said firmly. As if he wasn't wired enough, without giving him sugary treats.

She stopped cold as they walked through the door. Across the crowded lobby stood Gallagher, looking like a mountain surrounded by chattering Japanese. She had thought that he would be able to manage the sleigh-ride, somehow.

He spotted her. His eyes narrowed to sapphire slits.

'I don't care what you want,' she interrupted Kenny, taking his arm firmly and moving towards Gallagher. The moment of truth had arrived—or might have arrived, except that Kenny impatiently shook free of her grip and made a beeline for the confectionery stall.

The Japanese were beaming recognition and waving greetings at her. She hesitated, and then, with a reluctant look at Kenny's back, went over to say a quick hello.

'I see now why you couldn't possibly have given me a hand tonight,' Gallagher said. His voice was smooth and pleasant. The sarcasm of his message was intended only for her.

Her chin went up. 'I made a promise,' she stated with cold lack of apology. 'It's not as if you gave me three days' notice that you would need help.'

Looking at him, she suddenly knew that now was the time. See if he could meet Kenny and still smile that cold, cynical smile. Then he might at least understand the full extent of her responsibility. He might be less inclined to see her limitations as a personal insult. Suddenly, she did not dread this moment. She wanted it.

'When he's finished buying popcorn, I'd like you to meet——' She broke off when, out of the corner of her eye, she caught a movement in the queue. She turned to see that Kenny had grown impatient and was barging his way to the front. Once there, he loudly demanded popcorn, two Cokes, liquorice, a chocolate bar and——

'Excuse me,' she said hastily. Damn Kenny! He didn't even have any money.

She reached him, took one look at his mutinous face, and sighed. She was aware that he was fully intending to make a scene if he was denied so much as a jujube. Perhaps he would manage to be pleasant to Gallagher if she placated him now. She paid for the monstrous amount of junk piled in front of him. But when she turned back to the lobby Gallagher and his clients had disappeared into the cinema.

The Roxy was a wonderful old cinema that had been painstakingly restored. Thankfully the seats Kenny coveted—semi-box seats, set off from the others by a low, rounded wall—were still available. Charlie herded Kenny into one, luxuriating in the relative privacy and leg-room. She glanced around, pinpointing Gallagher's location, so that she could find him easily after the show and introduce him to Kenny.

The lights came down, and the movie proved to be every bit as dreadful as Charlie had feared it would be. It was billed as a spy thriller, but it seemed to feature half-naked women romping about the screen. Kenny began to react to the junk food just as she had suspected he would, and he began to squirm, thump his feet, and finally bounce up and down in his chair despite her hissed warnings. Her head was beginning to hurt, and Kenny began to comment loudly on the show.

She whacked him warningly on the arm, but the comments continued, and the scenes being played out in front of them continued to sizzle. Finally, when Kenny crowed something particularly vulgar, she dismissed her plan to meet Gallagher afterwards, seized Kenny by the arm, yanked him to his feet, and hauled him out of the cinema, out of the front doors, and headed him towards home.

He was surprisingly complacent. 'I'm sorry,' he told her contritely as he came into her room to say goodnight to her. 'I was very bad.'

'Very,' she agreed, but she went from being ready to kill him, to being charmed by him. As always.

Gallagher sat looking at the two empty seats, seething. He had been absolutely stunned to see Charlie with a man. Somehow it had never occurred to him that she might have a boyfriend. It made him furious that she had allowed that kiss of a week ago to ever take place. How dared she engage in that kind of activity if she was committed elsewhere? OK, it had been spontaneous. But she had seen it coming. Her golden eyes had been half-closed and sensuous, her tongue had been tickling the edge of her lips. She could have stopped it. Not only hadn't she stopped it, but she had given every bit as good as she got.

And that damned kiss still lingered on his lips and in his mind. She had tasted pure and fresh, like a snowflake melting on the tip of his tongue. Every time he looked at her he yearned to taste those lips again. Even when he wasn't looking at her, he saw her. The wide, intelligent eyes. The tangled mane of her hair. Yes, the soft, tantalising bow of her lips. He had known she meant trouble. Known it from the first time he had laid eyes on her. And hired her anyway, fool that he was.

Hired her despite the fact that she had given him

hell at that first interview for his inadvertent
admission that men found younger women
attractive. And then tonight she had waltzed in on
the arm of a man who, though Gallagher had only
seen him briefly, didn't appear to be a day over
twenty. And women accused men of applying
double standards. Ha!

His eyes had drifted to them once or twice
during the show. He had seen her leaning over
and whispering to him, seen her give him a playful
smack on the shoulder. And they had got up
during a very graphic sex scene and left. He
couldn't prevent himself from thinking the very
ugly thought that they couldn't wait to get home.

Gallagher sighed, wondering why the hell he
cared. She had an alluring physical presence—one
that, unfortunately, he was always aware of. A
masculine weakness, nothing more.

The problem was that you didn't just have an
affair with a woman like that, and get her out of
your system. A woman like that would take
energy—mental, physical, emotional. A woman
like that would take *everything*. She would never
be satisfied with leftovers—with less than a man's
full presence. Challenging, yes, but draining, too,
and that was if you were lucky enough to survive
the sharp edges.

No, Charlie James was not his kind of woman.
He liked women who were softer. Less assertive.
Who didn't keep him on his toes, like a boxer
waiting for a punch. Who didn't make him think
about every word before he said it.

Suddenly, and unhappily, he wasn't certain if he liked what that said about him.

Gallagher's face was unreadable and remote the next morning when they saw each other. Charlie refused to let that stop her.

'Did you enjoy your evening?' she asked tentatively.

'No!' he snapped.

'I had to leave early,' she pressed on. 'Otherwise I would have liked you to meet Kenny. He's——'

'Look, lady,' Gallagher cut her off, 'I don't give a damn about your personal life. You've made it perfectly clear that all you want to do is fly the helicopter. That's fine by me. More than fine. That's just great.'

Charlie stared at him, feeling a horrible, tell-tale sting behind her lashes. She had planned this moment so carefully—wanted so badly for him to know this guarded part of herself, of her life.

She had almost trusted him. Well, he did not deserve her trust. And he certainly did not deserve her tears.

'Which group is going up first?' she asked tightly, turning her attention quickly away from the stone-like cast of his face. Damn him for ever revealing he had a different side from this.

And damn her, for foolishly entertaining the notion that the side seen more infrequently might be the more real one.

CHAPTER SIX

'Do you mind?' Gallagher snapped, when his shoulder brushed Charlie's as he was loading skis.

Charlie felt her temper sizzle. It was her first morning back at work after two weeks off. She had hoped that two weeks would mellow them both. Give them a chance to step back and get things in perspective. Give them a chance to recover from the tension, the physical strain those last two weeks of working together had put on them. It had been exhausting—wearing the frigid mask of uncaring, parrying indifference with indifference. Fighting back the desire to point out a windborne eagle to him, or the way the light had hit a certain outcropping. Fighting back simple sharing words about sky, snow, sunshine.

She had hoped that the two weeks' respite would give *him* a chance to figure out why he was always going for her throat. Figure out why he was so completely unreasonable towards her. Now, it was obvious he had not used the time constructively. She, however, had.

She had swept him from her mind completely. Well, almost completely. It was true that, in her unguarded moments, her mind occasionally drifted. To sapphire eyes. To a lone figure conquering a windswept mountain. To the way his jacket moulded over the broad swell of his shoulders, the way his ski-pants hugged the muscular line of his leg.

Occasionally, in an unguarded moment, she had found herself trying to peer inside him. Trying to decipher his coldness, his moodiness. Despite the people who surrounded him, the relentless activity of his life, there was a basic aloofness about him that made her see a man lonely and alone. See a man who guarded his vulnerability with chilling vigilance.

Occasionally, in an unguarded moment, she felt an aching and odd tenderness for that man. An aching desire to break through his barriers, to soar into the brilliance of that soul she had seen bared.

Just occasional, unguarded moments of craziness. Of pure insanity. Moments that she crushed as ruthlessly as she would crush fat, slimy bugs, as soon as she realised that she had let herself slip again.

Yes, she had used her two weeks constructively. Or so she had thought. Until she had seen him, and her heart had leapt in her throat, and she had felt the colour unfurling in her cheeks like bright red flags.

And then he had crushed her leaping heart as ruthlessly as if *it* were the fat, slimy bug. With a look of schooled indifference, with a harsh thread running through his every word to her.

She faced him now, speaking under her breath so that the group of skiers wouldn't hear her.

'Look, buddy, if you have a problem, kindly get it out in the open.'

'I'm not your buddy, and I don't have a problem,' he returned coldly. 'Do you?'

'Me?' she squeaked. 'I most definitely do not!'

'Fine, then. Get to work.'

As if she had been dallying while he worked himself into a sweat! She wanted to grab the ski-pole from his hand and hit him over the head with it—again, and again, and again. She wanted to tell him that, since he was so godlike that he didn't like to be touched by mere mortals, he would have no trouble flying the helicopter by himself. Then she wanted to turn on her heel, walk away and never come back. Hurt him, as he was hurting her, even if from his perspective the only hurt would be the mad scramble to find a new pilot. Reactions of passion, she realised, astonished. No, her two weeks off had not been so terribly constructive, after all.

She bit her lip, and turned with a strained smile to the skier holding out his equipment to her.

'You two married?' he asked with a grin.

'Never!' she said emphatically.

'Great! How about dinner with me tonight, doll?'

She almost repeated her emphatic 'never'. She almost told *him* to fly the helicopter. 'Doll'! Instead she held her smile, wondering what had ever compelled her to take a job that required diplomacy.

'I'm afraid that's impossible. I have a family.'

Sort of a family, she added to herself—certainly enough of one to want to discourage idiots like this.

'Really? How old are your kids?'

'There's only one. He's about twelve.' OK, she was stretching it, and it disagreed with her scrupulously honest nature. But she couldn't very well back out now. She grabbed his skis and motioned for him to move by.

'Your kid's twelve?' Gallagher asked, his normal remoteness displaced by his incredulous tone.

Now what had she started? 'On his good days,' she mumbled evasively. She would not accept this invitation to reveal more about herself, thank you very much, even if she did not like to be misleading. Gallagher had made it perfectly clear that he did not want to hear any of the details of her personal life once before. Trusting him with titbits from her life would be like trusting a shark with a shrimp!

'You were sixteen when you had your kid?'

His tone was soft, strangely caring. She looked at him, to see that his eyes had softened, too. How she had wanted a moment like this between them! So that they could begin mending fences. And it might have been, if the look that softened his eyes had been anything but pity.

But Charlie abhorred pity, and she had been on the receiving end of it a great deal because of Kenny. If she told him the truth right now, she suspected that the look that so wounded her pride and dignity would deepen. That was not what she wanted from Gallagher. She did not know what she did want from him, but it wasn't that.

'What's Cherry doing here?' Charlie asked, glad for the distraction provided by the minibus arriving. 'Her group isn't scheduled to go for another forty-five minutes.'

Cherry approached them hurriedly. She flashed Charlie a 'welcome back' smile, that didn't hide the anxiety in her eyes. 'We've got a hot one,' she explained briefly, before turning to Gallagher.

Gallagher already seemed to know exactly what the problem was. His eyes were narrowed dangerously on a handsome young man outfitted in very expensive gear. Charlie followed his gaze. The man's expression was scowling and sulky, and clearly spelled trouble.

'He says he won't go with me,' Cherry said in a rushed undertone. 'He said my group was too slow for him yesterday. I can't handle him anyway, Gallagher. He just won't listen to me.'

'Hell,' Gallagher breathed. 'He's barely intermediate as it is.' He sighed. 'You're right, though. He'd better be some place where I can keep my eye on him.'

The man in question approached cockily. 'I should have been put with the experts in the first place,' he informed Gallagher. 'What kind of Mickey Mouse operation is this?'

'It's been looked after, Mr Damon,' Gallagher said, with admirable restraint.

Damon looked disappointed. Charlie suspected that he was looking for trouble, and having difficulty finding it. He noticed her, and leered.

'And who's the sweet thing?'

Gallagher's eyes had been dangerous before. Now the light in them could only be described as killing. An interesting reaction, Charlie thought, her squashed heart reviving a bit.

His calm tone belied the message of his eyes. 'This is our pilot for today, Charlie James.'

Damon scowled. 'Where's the guy who flew yesterday?'

'It's his day off.' Impatience was weaving its way through the calm, now. 'Charlie is as competent a pilot as Leon, perhaps more so. Now, if you'd kindly join my group——'

Charlie barely had time to appreciate the rare compliment.

'Get the other guy back. I ain't flying with no babe at the wheel.'

'Don't, then,' Gallagher challenged tersely, and folded his arms across his chest.

Damon smiled a crafty smile, and nodded at the milling skiers. 'These people are my friends. I don't go, they don't go. One word's all it would take.'

Charlie read the set of Gallagher's face, and knew the word was going to be said. She laid a staying hand on Gallagher's arm. She had a lot of experience in dealing with Kenny. And a lot of experience in dealing with stubborn men. The two combined would be more than a match for Damon.

She smiled sweetly at him. 'Do you ski because you like the danger, Mr Damon?' she asked, her

tone awed. Out of the corner of her eye she saw
Gallagher give her a disgusted look.

Damon, however, thrust forward his chest and
grinned. 'You betcha, babe.'

The sweet smile dropped from her lips. 'Some
people seek danger because they're really not very
brave. Did you know that? They're trying to prove
something. But sometimes they also look for
excuses along the way. A set of circumstances that
would allow them to bow out and save face at the
same time.' Her voice was soft—polite but lethal.
'Excuses like not liking to fly with a woman. The
least dangerous thing you'll do today, Mr Damon,
is board that helicopter. I'm very interested in
whether you'll do it or not.'

Damon hesitated, scowled at her, and then
brushed by them and boarded the helicopter.

Cherry was looking at her with her mouth
hanging open. Gallagher's eyes were fastened on
her with amazement. And then with respect, and
finally, unexpectedly, with mirth.

'You're one tough lady,' he said slowly.

'When I have to be,' she returned, stiffly.
Tough? Was it because he thought she was tough
that he was so callous towards her?

'Remind me not to cross you,' he teased her.

The teasing note was so unexpected, so warm
after the long chill, that she melted, despite
herself. 'You already have,' she warned him, but
there was sudden laughter in her voice, too.

Their gazes locked for a long time. Laughter-
filled. Appreciative. Asking and giving

forgiveness.

But she reminded herself how utterly foolish it was to leave herself open to this man, reminded herself how she had paid for breaking her rule already.

He remembered seeing her with her boyfriend at the cinema.

The familiar coldness settled in—and was made even colder for that brief sighting of the sun.

'Did you check the straps?' he asked shortly a few minutes later as he took the seat beside her.

She sent him an exasperated look. 'Of course.'

'Then what the hell are you waiting for?'

Maybe, she thought wearily, even pity would have been better than this.

'I'm glad I caught you before you left,' she said to him over the phone the next morning.

'Don't you dare tell me you're sick. Have you seen the snow we got last night? It'll be the best skiing of the year today!'

His boyish enthusiasm was just appealing enough that she managed to forgive his lack of concern for her health.

'I'm not sick,' she said drily. 'My driveway has fallen victim to the ploughs again.'

'Is that all? I'll be there in fifteen minutes.'

It occurred to her, as she sat beside him in his truck, that she really could have called Cherry and got a lift in one of the minibuses. She wondered why she hadn't thought of that. Why would she spend an extra minute in this boorish man's company when she didn't have to? Except, she had to admit, he wasn't being his usual boorish self this morning. His enthusiasm over the snow was overriding that—until they came to the last curve in the road before the airport. A truck had overturned and the way was completely blocked. The Royal Canadian Mounted Police were on the spot, and one of them ambled over.

'Good morning, Gallagher.'

'Until ten seconds ago, it was a fairly decent morning,' Gallagher muttered, glaring at the overturned truck.

The police officer laughed. 'We'll have this all cleared up in half an hour or so——'

'Half an hour?' Gallagher exploded.

'Say the Serenity Prayer,' Charlie suggested sweetly.

Gallagher glared at her. 'Do you need a hand, Michael?'

'No, save yourself for the slopes.' He winked at Charlie with sympathy, and walked away.

'Maybe we should go and get a coffee or something,' Charlie suggested tentatively when Gallagher continued to glower at the road as though his will could move the wreckage out of the way.

'They might have it cleared up sooner.'

'Gallagher, it's half an hour. Out of a lifetime. Lighten up.'

He let his eyes drift wistfully to the fresh snow visible on the mountain peaks, then he sighed, and grinned at her, a trifle humbly. 'Am I being that rotten?'

'Yes, not that it's anything new.'

'At least the police are here.'

'I beg your pardon?'

'After half an hour in this cab together, one of us could end up dead.'

She took a deck of cards out of her bag, and fanned them in his face. 'Especially if I win?' she taunted.

A glimmer of a smile touched his lips. 'Especially then,' he agreed. 'Deal.'

Some moments later, Charlie said tentatively, 'Gallagher, maybe this is a good time to talk about why we're not getting along.'

He frowned at his cards. 'We're getting along. We'd be getting along a lot better if you weren't winning. You play blackjack like a man.'

She sighed. 'You're avoiding the issue.'

'What is the issue? And why do women always do this? Wait until they have a captive audience, and then decide it's time to talk.'

'I think it's the only time they can nail you guys down. And did you just notice how I can't win? I play blackjack like a man, and that's a fault, and I trap you into talking, like a woman, and that's a fault.'

'I guess you just have a lot of faults.' He glanced at her face. 'Should I call Michael back over now?'

'Maybe,' she said. She was feeling a bit murderous.

He slowly set down the cards, and looked at her intently. She could feel her cheeks start to heat from the intensity of his scrutiny. And from something else—from the way those eyes, darkened to midnight-blue, had trailed over her hair like a physical touch, and were now fastened on her lips.

She should look away, she told herself. But, after all, she had started this. Besides, she had discovered that she was powerless to look away.

He leaned towards her, as if drawn on an invisible thread. Again she was aware of what she *should* do. She should back away. Laugh. Put words in between them. And again she could not do it, could not break the mesmerising spell of those eyes, could not deny her own aching need to feel his lips once more on hers.

His lips touched hers, tentatively—as if he would find some answer he sought there. The softness lasted for one beat of a hummingbird's wing, and was gone. A savage groan emitted from him, he tangled his hands in her hair, and pulled her into the fury of his kiss.

It was a summer storm. Thunder cracked and lightning split the heavens. It was magnificent. Exhilarating. Awesomely powerful. Frightening. His kisses were like hard, merciless rain, sizzling across the heated surface of her skin. At first she was just an innocent bystander caught in a torrential downpour. But then it changed. She was the storm. Its passion was coming from within her, not from outside her. They were joining, two untameable forces, fired with electrical energy, swirling around each other, crackling, sizzling, hissing. And then melting. Surrendering. The fury dying and giving way to the stillness that followed the storm. Washing them in a silent calm, touching tormented souls with a promise of peace . . .

Gallagher tore his lips from hers and shoved her away from him. His mighty shoulders were heaving, and he turned his face from her. When he turned back, his face was composed, save for the strained line about his mouth.

'There it is, Charlie,' he finally said, his voice gravelled. 'That's why we're not getting along.'

She stared at him, wide-eyed. The trembling within her was only just beginning to subside, and it was being replaced by a cold chill. As if she had indeed been swept away by the magnificence of a summer storm, but now was left cold, and drenched to the skin. Uncertain, now that the magnificence was fading in the distance, if the price she had paid to be a part of it was not too high.

'I don't understand,' she whispered.

He gave her an impatient look. 'It's there, Charlie. It's always there.' He looked grimly out of the window, his voice cold and controlled. 'And it's never going to go away.'

She wanted to press him, wanted to play innocent, and insist he tell her *what* was there. But she couldn't. Because she knew. Something so strong between them, it was tangible. She could reach out with her fingertips and touch it. A physical, a chemical reaction to one another. Made even more abhorrent, to him, no doubt, as well as to her, because it overrode the fact that they could both rationally acknowledge that they were too different. Intellectually they could both acknowledge that they had too much to lose by following that feeling. Too much to risk. Too many scars, too much history.

And yet he was right. It was still there, shimmering in the air between them.

A rap on the window.

'OK, lovebirds,' the RCMP constable told them with a knowing grin. 'Road's open.'

She glanced at Gallagher. The stern line around his mouth was white. And she knew that things were going to be worse than ever.

That night Charlie sat beside Kenny, blankly watching the TV, her mind whirling as she tried to figure out what to do. Today had put them on the edge, she thought. The very edge. Of danger. Of discovery. How easy it would be to throw herself over, into a world fraught with the unknown. Into a world of risk and daring that might eventually lead her to the promise she thought she had seen at the very core of this man. But she had glimpsed that promise so infrequently. Was it really there, or just a rationalisation for the strong physical pull she felt towards him?

It was there. She knew it. He knew it. And as long as they continued to work together it would continue to surface. They would be forced to make the decision to ignore it, to walk away from it, again and again. Only how long could that last—before one of them, or both of them, capitulated?

Decisions. She thought of Paul, for the first time in months. Her decision back then had been absolutely without option. As painful as walking barefoot over jagged ice, but still a decision without alternative. But her feelings for Paul had been childish, romance untempered with any form of realism. There was nothing childish, or fairy-tale-like, about the storm of conflicting emotion Gallagher stirred within her. Anger, confusion, desire and tenderness were all components. It was not like what she had felt for Paul. It was not comfortable, and yet oddly enough it was both more compelling and more real.

Her gaze flicked to Kenny. If Gallagher asked her to choose—she shut off the thought with brutal force, but not quickly enough. She had just contemplated betraying Kenny and, from the twist in her gut, the contemplation felt as great as having actually committed the sin.

She stood up and turned off the TV. 'Time for bed, tiger.'

'I'm not a baby!' Kenny screamed at her. He turned it back on, and sat there mutinously.

She realised that she had known this was coming, had seen signs of it for weeks. There was a baffling restlessness in Kenny. A stubbornness in him that hadn't been present before.

She realised, too, that she didn't have the energy for it right now. She couldn't handle a fight with him. 'Turn off the set when you're through,' she said, and wearily climbed the stairs.

It wasn't *really* Kenny, anyway, she thought, in bed. It was his relationship with Mike, Tanya's brother, that seemed to be at the heart of these disturbing changes in her cousin.

With regret, because she had come to like Tanya very much, she spoke to her the next morning.

Tanya listened to her solemnly, and then shook her head slowly. 'Charlie, I don't think the problem is Mike, so much as it's that Mike shows Kenny what he could be.'

'Tanya, Kenny's not as advanced as your brother.'

'It took Mike a lot of hard work to become that "advanced". He's not doing a thing that Kenny couldn't do, with training, and hard work, and support.'

'That's not true, and it's not fair to let Kenny think it's true.'

'Let him go, Charlie. Let him test his wings.'

'No,' Charlie whispered. 'You just don't understand.'

Tanya shook her head, her eyes gentle on Charlie's face. 'What would be wrong with letting him try a job?'

'He tried to work once. It was a disaster. It broke his heart.'

'So now you're going to protect him. From broken hearts? That's part of this business called living, Charlie.'

For some reason the words struck her as a double-edged sword. It wasn't just Kenny she desperately tried to protect from broken hearts. Perhaps that elusive 'something' that she always felt was missing from her life wasn't romance at all. Perhaps it was that, somewhere along the way, she had forfeited her ability to risk, forfeited her opportunity to ever live life as fully as it was meant to be lived.

'Just think about it,' Tanya suggested softly.

She found herself agreeing. But it just meant that there was one more situation in her life that was left unresolved. And her life was beginning to feel like a collection of unresolved conflicts.

Perhaps the real resolution was going to be to leave Revelstoke. It was not working out as she had hoped for Kenny. It was not working out as she had hoped for herself. Her trial period with High Heaven was nearly over. Should she leave voluntarily, instead of waiting for the axe to fall?

She was running again, she realised. Running from risk. She also realised that she was tired, so tired, of running.

CHAPTER SEVEN

GALLAGHER drove slowly through downtown Revelstoke. Grizzly Plaza looked merry. Christmas lights blinked from colourful awnings. Carollers chirped cheer from under the bright red dome of the bandstand. Shoppers bustled between banks of snow. Some child had even hung garlands around the necks of the three life-size bronze grizzly bears that guarded the entrance to the cobblestoned plaza.

A perfect Christmas scene, he thought, unmoved. Christmas was only three days away. He didn't feel like Christmas. He didn't feel anything but tired. He had even fobbed off entertaining tonight.

Because I would have killed Damon if I had to spend one more second with him, he thought. Probably would have killed him already, if it hadn't been for Charlie. She had a knack for keeping the troublemaker in line.

Still, there had been difficult groups before. Plenty of them. Why was it so different this time? Why was it wearing him down, sapping his energy, making him impatient and irritable? Because of her, he supposed. Charlie. Damn her. He had decided it would take a lot of energy to get involved with a woman like that. Now, he was discovering, it seemed to take just as much energy *not to*.

And there they were again, Gallagher thought blackly. Why did he have to see *them* tonight? Charlie's face, red-cheeked, shining out of the crowd. *The* guy with her, their arms laden with parcels. Merry Christmas. Ha-ha.

Since that night at the movies, he seemed to see them all over town together. Just by themselves. He saw them, at a distance, in the downtown stores, getting groceries, out for walks. Once, he'd seen them chasing each other through the waist-high snow of the deserted Queen Elizabeth Park. He knew he should have kept driving, but he hadn't. He had stopped and watched them from a distance, watched their joy-filled faces as they cavorted like young puppies, heard the faint tinkle of her laughter.

And he'd felt so angry. What right had she to be happy, when she was at the root of the worst confusion he'd felt in his life?

He didn't want her. She was sharp-tongued, shrewish and entirely too sure of herself. She was, in a nutshell, not very feminine. But, if he didn't want her, he had to admit that he didn't want anybody else to have her, either.

Didn't want anybody else to tame that independent spirit, to share her strength, to make her laugh that warming laugh, to make the sun rise in her eyes.

Gallagher became aware that he was still

watching them, still frowning. Hell! He put his foot on to the accelerator. He didn't want her to spot him sitting in his truck staring at her. He braked as suddenly as he had sped up.

The couple had stopped abruptly, and were having a heated discussion. Gallagher unwound his window, unabashedly listening to them. Maybe normally he wouldn't have. Only, the hair on the back of his neck was tingling with a strong sixth sense.

'Chuck!' the guy screamed at her, throwing down one bag and then the other. Gallagher heard glass breaking, registered and hated the fact that *he* had a pet name for her in the same instant. He saw the man's movement, sensed the anger in it, and sprang from his truck.

He wasn't fast enough. He saw her boyfriend push her, send her flying into the snow. For the first time in his life he felt entirely out of control—his rage causing his vision to be entirely washed in red.

He tackled the man from behind, feeling satisfied at the frightened whimper of surprise that escaped him as he tumbled. Propelled by rage, Gallagher straddled him and lifted his fist, in the back of his mind hearing Charlie's startled cry, her fearful scream.

'No, Gallagher, no!'

But, if anything, her loyalty, and the note of pleading in her voice, only enraged him more. The guy deserved to have his lights turned out. He deserved to be beaten to a pulp. His reaction had nothing to do with his confused mixture of feelings about Charlie—he was almost positive of that. It sprang from his belief that men did not push women around—not in the privacy of their homes, not on public streets.

Gallagher could hear Charlie starting to cry and, out of the corner of his eye, he could see her struggling to get on her feet, could sense her urgency to stop that which nothing was going to stop now.

His fist frozen over his shoulder, Gallagher focused on the face before him, registered the fear, and felt a primal satisfaction in it. He was not surprised that a coward lurked beneath the bully. He could feel the muscles in his arm bunching, the pure power of his fury coiling along the length of his arm. He swung.

His fist stopped an inch short of the man's face. Gallagher's arm shook from the force he'd had to exert to stop that blow. He felt the blood-red recede from his eyes. He wasn't even sure exactly what had stopped him. Something in the eyes, and a sudden sick feeling at the bottom of his belly that he was wrong—terribly, dreadfully wrong.

Those eyes locked on his with such dread, with all the terror of a cornered animal, were not the eyes of a man. They were the eyes of a child.

He felt dazed. His fist dropped impotently to his side, and he gave way easily under Charlie's shove. He rose to his feet, staring at them.

She was gathering the man-boy into her arms, rocking him like a mother, crooning soothing words into his ears. And he was crying now, huge tears slithering down his cheeks, his fists clutching at Charlie's jacket as though he would never let her go.

'Chuckie,' he sobbed. 'Chuckie, Chuckie, Chuckie.'

Finally, she looked up at him. Gallagher expected to see anger in her eyes. He was prepared for it—and deserved it. All the assumptions. All the silent accusations he'd made. He held his breath. She could kill him with her eyes right now.

The breath released slowly. There was no censure in those huge, golden eyes. Just an intensely beautiful light that could have brought him to his knees.

'Oh, lord, Charlie,' Gallagher murmured hoarsely. 'What have I done?'

The man-boy slid him a wary look. 'You were going to hit me,' he accused, and his voice trailed down to a wail of remembered fear.

Slowly the sobs subsided, Gallagher standing there feeling helpless and like a fool, as Charlie sat in the snow rocking and crooning and stroking. Finally, gently, she pushed the boy from her embrace and tugged him to his feet.

'Gallagher, this is my cousin, Kenny.'

Kenny hid behind her, having to crouch to do so.

'He won't hurt you, Kenny,' she soothed. 'He made a mistake.'

'I'm sorry,' Gallagher addressed the boy softly.

'You can't know how sorry I am.'

'I don't like you,' Kenny reported stubbornly.

'Now, Kenny——'

Gallagher held up a hand, silencing her. 'I don't like myself very much right now, either, Ken.'

'Because you nearly hurt me?'

'Yes, because I nearly hurt you. Charlie, I'll give you and Ken a lift home. I think we should talk.'

Charlie felt ill at ease with Gallagher seated comfortably at the table in her small kitchen. The room was too small for him. He filled it, became its focal point, with his arm hooked casually over the back of his chair, his long legs stretched out beneath the table. She was aware of his eyes resting on her carefully turned back. She worked with him, and flying was far more complicated than making tea. And yet now she felt awkward and clumsy. She dropped the sugar. She spilled the milk. She wondered what a man—especially a man like Gallagher—would think of a woman who was more at ease in a cockpit than a kitchen.

Finally, she set the teapot between them, pulled out a chair, and settled on it in a kneeling position, unaware that her posture was one that suggested she might get up and run at any minute. She could faintly hear the cartoons in the next room, where Kenny sat watching them.

'Speak,' Gallagher requested softly, taking a sip of his tea, those sapphire eyes locked on hers.

'About what?' she asked carelessly, nervously studying the tea-leaves in her cup.

'For starters, I keep expecting a twelve-year-old—yours—to come bounding into the room.'

She looked at him with genuine bafflement.

He sighed. 'You told me you had a dependant. Then you mentioned that your child was twelve. Is there a child?'

She smiled weakly. 'No. Kenny's my dependant, and I'm afraid he does act about twelve, so in that moment I used him as an excuse to get out of doing something I didn't want to do.'

Gallagher nodded solemnly. 'Why didn't you just tell me, Charlie?' he finally asked softly.

'You don't give a damn about my personal life, remember?'

He was silent for a moment. 'I saw you around town with Ken a couple of times. I thought he was your boyfriend.'

His eyes were suddenly hooded, and she was uncertain what to make of the words. Surely that couldn't be the reason he'd been on such a short fuse, so unfeeling, so unfair, so . . . untouchable? He couldn't have been jealous? Gallagher? But if he had been . . .

Something stirred gently in her heart, but she stopped it. If he had been jealous that only made life more complicated, more threatening. More of a risk.

'I just didn't see that it was any of your business. I just didn't think that my personal problems would be of the least bit of interest to you.' She regretted her choice of phrase immediately, because something in Gallagher's eyes flickered at the word 'problem'. Pity?

'If you had unusual circumstances that prevented you from giving as much to the company as I sometimes expect, I think it would have been only fair, to both of us, if you had let me know.'

She felt deflated, when she should have felt relieved. Not jealousy, after all. His concern was for his company. For the employee-employer relationship.

'Perhaps I should have told you.' She studied her tea again. 'It's just that sometimes it's very difficult for me to explain about Kenny. Most people don't understand. There are still a lot of prejudices and stigmas attached to the handicapped, and particularly to the mentally handicapped.'

The scar leapt suddenly along his jawline. 'And I struck you as a person with narrow-minded prejudices? Did and still do?'

'Certainly not,' she replied, an edge of sarcasm creeping into her voice. 'You don't have any prejudices. You were dead set against hiring a woman pilot. But prejudices? Where would I get such a ridiculous notion?'

He sucked in his breath. 'That's long behind us, Charlie, and below the belt. Nobody is without prejudices. The mark of the kind of person they are is whether they can overcome them. I did. Shouldn't that have earned me a measure of your trust?'

'Did you ever overcome your reservations about

hiring me, Gallagher? If you did, I haven't felt it. It's December. I've been expecting my walking papers.'

He looked troubled, ran a hand through his tangle of black curls. 'Professionally, Charlie, I have no problems. You're a damn good pilot.'

'Thank you,' she said stiffly, 'I didn't know that.'

'See?' he said, softly. 'There it is, right there. You don't react the way I expect a woman to react. You're supposed to get coy and grateful when I say something nice to you.'

She was genuinely puzzled. 'But I *am* a good pilot. I don't need you to tell me the obvious to make it true.'

'I know that. I think I even like it, *sometimes*. But I don't know how to relate to you. It's like you've thrown out the rule-book.'

'I didn't realise there was a rule-book!'

'Of course there is. Nothing that's written down, but a whole set of culturally defined rules about how men and women are supposed to relate. But you don't play by it.'

'Couldn't you just relate to me as a person? Forget gender?'

'Oh, Charlie,' he said with a slight grin, 'look in the mirror some time. It would take a bigger man than me to forget you were a woman.'

'Oh,' she said, both uncomfortable and pleased. She could feel a self-conscious blush suffusing her cheeks.

For a moment they sat in silence. Her blush

intensified as he studied her with such frank masculine appreciation. Intensified again as she realised that she was studying him with just as frank feminine appreciation.

He was right, she realised, there were rules. Rules that could be obliterated in a second by the chemistry that was bubbling in her stomach. And in his, if the intensity in those darkening eyes was any indication.

'Tell me about you and Kenny,' he invited softly. Was he deliberately breaking the tense awareness that was beginning to stir between them?

Charlie hesitated, nodded, and took a deep breath.

'Kenny and I grew up like a brother and a sister. My parents were theatre people—actors, who never quite made the big time. They travelled, following dinner circuits, and Shakespearian festivals. For the first few years of my life, I travelled with them. I hated it. I was never in the same school. I never had the same friends. We kept weird hours, and associated with some pretty strange people.

'I read a lot, and I knew that it wasn't normal, that a different kind of life existed, and I was always dreaming of this perfect, normal family. Then, one Christmas, we were invited to stay with my Uncle Henry and Aunt Joss. They were so wonderfully normal,' she recalled dreamily. 'They had this big, wonderful, robust family, and I loved every second of being with them. We were there for two weeks. The last week I cried every night thinking about going back on the road. My misery wasn't as private a thing as I would have thought. My parents noticed it. Aunt Joss and Uncle Henry noticed it. They wanted to take me. Actually wanted to,' she remembered fondly, 'and, though my parents were reluctant at first, they agreed to try it for a year.'

She was lost in thought now, unaware that a faint pain laced her words and hollowed her eyes. 'For the first year they called often, sent me things, came to visit. After that, things just tapered off.' She stopped, aware of her sadness, and smiled in defiance of it. 'At this point we exchange Christmas cards and not too much else. But they're a part of me, still, even if I haven't been around them much. I inherited a spirit of adventure from them that was completely alien to my aunt and uncle. In a way, I ended up with the best of both worlds. Stability from Joss and Henry, imagination and a sense of fun and adventure from my parents.'

'What happened to your aunt and uncle?' Gallagher prodded softly.

'They died. Aunt Joss died, too young, of cancer. Uncle Henry just kind of gave up and followed. At that time Kenny and I were the only ones still left at home. I've always been really close to him. Uncle Henry and I discussed it one night. We knew I was the right one, even though I was the youngest. They had a modest insurance policy. It went to me. It's a sad twist of fate, but it was the money from their insurance that allowed me to pursue my dream of becoming a pilot. I weighed it out carefully. The money was for Kenny, but forty thousand wasn't enough to last him very long. And I wasn't going to be able to support us both as an accounts clerk. So, I set myself up in a profession that would allow me to comfortably look after Kenny for the rest of his life. It's icing on the cake that I get to do something that I love to do.'

'You said it was a big family. Do they help you?'

'They're all older than him. They barely know him. They wanted to put him away somewhere. They wanted to——' She stopped, controlled her voice. 'It was unthinkable. I was the one prepared to take him—the one who wanted to. So I did. And we're doing just fine.'

Somehow his hand had come across the table and closed around hers. His grip was dry and strong and firm. She found herself looking at his hands, thinking they were beautiful. She reluctantly removed her hand from his, picked up her tea, met his eyes. They were beautiful, too.

'And that's that,' she said with a faked blitheness that didn't fool either of them.

'Life's been hard on you,' he said softly, unwanted sympathy mellowing his voice and his eyes.

She was reminded suddenly of something Tanya had said. Tanya had stayed for tea after work, as she often did, listening to tales of Charlie's day, telling her what she and Kenny had done . . .

Charlie teased her about reading tea-leaves and Tanya looked at her sombrely.

'With some people, it is not necessary to read palms, or leaves. With some people you read faces.'

Charlie wanted to pretend that she didn't care for such nonsense but, like most people, she was intrigued at the hint of mystery, at the vague suggestion that someone could tell her something about herself, her past, her future.

'And what do you see in my face?' she asked lightly.

The look Tanya gave her was searing and intense, her voice low and musical as she spoke.

'I see four dragons. I see desertion. I see death. I see betrayal.'

Charlie stared at her, stunned. Her parents had deserted her. Her aunt and uncle had died. Paul had betrayed her. 'And the fourth?' she queried lightly.

'The fourth lies within you, waiting to be slain.'

'That's ridiculous,' Charlie said firmly.

'Is it?'

Was it? 'Kenny has, no doubt, told you a great deal about us.'

'No. Kenny, Mike—they don't dwell much on what has been. Sometimes I think that's the lesson they have to teach us. That there is no past. And no future. Just now. Only this moment. It's funny—great spiritualists work very hard to arrive at a state of mind very close to what Kenny and

Mike already have.'

'That's very perceptive,' Charlie conceded slowly. She hesitated, gave up trying to appear indifferent. 'What else does my face tell you?'

'That you carry bitter burdens, and that you often question the path of your life. You see the lives of others unfolding without the tragedy and troubles you have seen, and it angers you that life is so easy for some, but not for you.'

Charlie could only stare at Tanya helplessly. Her most secret thoughts seemed to be on display.

'And?' she finally whispered.

'And,' Tanya said with a smile, 'life has made you incredibly strong. Strong enough that one day you will quit complaining that life's lessons are too hard, and instead you will ask, "What am I to learn from this?" And you will find that all along you learned. That you grew stronger. By stronger, I mean you learned to love, to be gentle, accepting, compassionate. When you are old, and you will grow very old, you will have that look in your eyes—that wondrous look of laughter and wisdom. That look that means you have seen the worst of life, and reckoned with it, allowed it to teach, instead of destroy. You think your suffering has been without reason? No, Charlie, no. You were chosen because you are one of the few. The very few.'

Despite herself, Charlie found herself completely entranced by the soothing, melodious voice. 'The very few who what?'

Again, that soft, wise smile. 'One of the very

few who will know heaven on this earth.'

Charlie forced herself to laugh. 'Oh, sure!'

Tanya just shrugged, and smiled . . .

'Charlie, where are you?'

She looked blankly at Gallagher, as she came back to the present, and then grinned. 'Heaven only knows,' she muttered.

Kenny came in. 'Can I have some more hot chocolate?'

Charlie got up to get it for him.

'Come and join us for a minute,' Gallagher requested softly.

Kenny gave him a wary look, sidled over and slid down into a chair. 'You almost hit me,' he accused.

'Yes, I did. And I'd like to explain myself, if you'll let me.'

'I didn't do nuthin'!' Kenny proclaimed loudly and defensively.

'Hmm. I thought I saw you push Charlie.'

'Well, she made me mad! The bags were heavy, and I wanted to sit down, and she wouldn't let me. And I wanted candy at the store, and she wouldn't get me none! And why did we have to walk? I was cold, too. My hands were cold.'

'I told you to wear mittens,' Charlie reminded him quietly from the counter, watching the interchange with wary interest. Kenny was still rattled. The situation was delicate. It would be so terribly easy for Gallagher to mean well, and to say exactly the wrong thing.

But Gallagher seemed to know exactly where he

was going and what he was doing.

'Ken,' he said, not following her example and using the more juvenile 'Kenny', 'when I look at you, do you know what I see? I see a strong, big man. Is that what you are?'

Kenny puffed up considerably, and shot Charlie a triumphant look as though he'd finally been recognised. 'Yes. I'm a man.'

'Because you're a man, Ken, you're bigger than Charlie, and stronger than her. Is that right?'

Kenny nodded smugly. 'Yup.'

'Well, there's a rule about being bigger and stronger than somebody, Ken. You have to watch your temper. You can't ever hit somebody, or push somebody, who is smaller and weaker than you. A man can't ever fight with a lady. Do you understand?' His voice was very stern. 'Not ever.'

'I didn't mean to,' Kenny said in a small voice.

'That's not good enough. You could have hurt her, and you could have hurt her badly—without meaning to. How would you have felt about that?'

Kenny's eyes were bright with tears that he was making a very manly effort to control. 'Awful,' he said softly.

'Man to man, now, Ken—I don't want anything like that to ever happen again. Is that understood?'

'Yessir.'

Charlie's mouth dropped open. She had never, ever heard Kenny use that particular phrase, and she saw his reluctant respect for Gallagher in it.

Gallagher dropped it. He didn't add anything or make threats. He simply expected to be understood and obeyed.

'Could I ask you something?' Kenny asked, his tone still cowed.

'Sure,' Gallagher said. 'Shoot.'

'If you aren't *ever* supposed to hit somebody smaller than you, how come you just about hit me?'

Charlie took in Gallagher's stunned face, and smothered her laughter. He had just learned lesson one about trying to tell Kenny something. That, for somebody who was not too bright, occasionally his logic was infallible.

Gallagher sent her a pleading look, but she just grinned. It was a hard question, and she wanted to see if he could retain the integrity and clarity of his original message while he tried to explain the little twist.

'Ken, that's a tough question,' he said, giving it his full respect. 'But I'll try to answer. Because Charlie is a woman, and I know you should never, ever be rough with a woman, I didn't really even notice your size, whether you were bigger or smaller than me. I just noticed that you were a man, and knew I had to stop you from hurting Charlie.'

Kenny nodded solemnly. 'I guess you like Charlie, don't you?'

'I guess I do,' Gallagher said thoughtfully, then changed the subject. 'Say, what are the two of you doing for Christmas?'

Kenny's delight died. 'Nuthin'. Charlie has to work.'

'I know,' Gallagher said, 'so do I. But how would the two of you like to come to my place for Christmas dinner, only on Christmas Eve?'

Kenny shrugged. 'Do you have a TV?'

'Not one that gets turned on on Christmas Eve,' Gallagher replied wryly. 'But I do have two horses and a sleigh, and a Christmas tree that needs chopping down.'

Kenny's face was always so open. He was looking at Gallagher with frank adoration. 'Could we, Chuckie, please?'

'I guess so,' she said. Gallagher was very good with Kenny. Too good. Her strongest reason for avoiding relationships was that people could not cope with, or accept, Kenny as a part of her life. And yet Gallagher was showing every sign of being a man who could cope with Kenny.

It was ridiculous for that to make hope rise in her like a butterfly shaking free of a cocoon, because so far Gallagher had shown no sign of being able to cope with *her*.

CHAPTER EIGHT

'WOW, you look gorgeous!' Kenny exclaimed. He looked around mischievously. 'Have you seen my cousin, Chuck, anywhere?'

Charlie laughed at Kenny's joke, but it reminded her that it had been some time since she had dressed formally. She wore a simple black silk cocktail-dress, accented with a gold belt, gold bracelets and gold earrings, all which drew subtle attention to the gold flecks in her eyes. She had added just a dusting of make-up, and then swept her hair up into a coil, leaving a few wisps to curl around her face and neck. Gorgeous? Well, probably not. But it was a dramatic difference from her usual canvas trousers and 'High Heaven' sweatshirt. And she was inordinately eager to see how Gallagher reacted to the difference—to her playing by the rules.

Half an hour later they arrived at Gallagher's. She noted, with a touch of disappointment, that his yard was full of cars, plus the two minibuses. Somehow, she had thought that the invitation was just for Kenny and herself. From the sounds coming from the house, Gallagher had a thousand people in there.

Gallagher answered the door himself. Charlie's

breath caught in her throat. He looked suave and faintly dangerous in formal black evening clothes. She could easily picture him as a river-boat gambler from days past.

He stared at her. 'You look very beautiful,' he finally said, a rough edge to his voice, as he stood back from the door.

'See what a few minutes of fiddling with your face can accomplish?' she returned lightly. He helped her off with her coat, and looked at her with discomforting appreciation.

'I wasn't quite expecting the crowd,' she commented, breaking her eyes from his and looking pointedly over his shoulder.

Reluctantly, he took his eyes from her, followed her gaze. 'Didn't I warn you? I guess I just assumed you knew. This place is a madhouse every Christmas Eve. The whole Cole clan gathers, plus I always invite the clients along. I discovered that even though people may choose to be away from home at Christmas, they aren't quite prepared for the reality of waking up on Christmas morning to the bare walls of a hotel-room. It doesn't matter how cynical people claim to be about Christmas. There used to be some pretty forlorn faces when I picked them up to go skiing. Now, I just have everybody camp out on the den floor. It seems to soothe the away-from-home blues.

'I was hoping, though,' he added, in a low voice, 'that you and I could sneak a few minutes to ourselves later. There are some things I want to talk to you about.'

She scanned his face, but found no evidence there that Gallagher was planning to be a Scrooge and fire her on Christmas Eve. Still, his voice made it sound important, and she felt a touch of anxiety.

Soon, however, both her initial disappointment at having found such a crowd, and her anxiety, dissipated. Several children ran by them, laughing. This, she thought, her eyes roaming the festive crowd, was what Christmas was supposed to be. It was the way it had always been when Aunt Joss was alive. She felt, suddenly and comfortably, as though she'd come home.

Gallagher took Charlie and Kenny around and made introductions. She knew the skiers, a group from France, but not Gallagher's family. Six brothers and sisters. Countless nieces and nephews, who obviously worshipped Gallagher.

'Kenny,' one of Gallagher's sisters called, 'we need a big tall guy to help us hang this garland.'

'They're very accepting, aren't they?' Charlie murmured, watching Bab give Kenny's shoulder a squeeze and point out where she wanted the garland.

'Very. Of course, they've had a lot of practice, putting up with me for all these years.'

'That explains it,' Charlie agreed wryly.

The 'menfolk' went out to get the tree, and Kenny was included in their ranks.

'Watch him with the axe,' Charlie whispered to Gallagher. 'He can be terribly clumsy.'

Gallagher cast her a look she didn't like very

much, but she quelled her instinctive defensive
feeling.

They arrived back, Kenny unscathed; the tree
was decorated, and dinner followed. Charlie felt as
though she had been around Gallagher and his
family all of her life. She'd missed the teasing and
support of family. So had Kenny, she realised,
watching him blossom under the warmth and
attention he was receiving. She was also seeing
Gallagher in a very different and flattering light.
He was very relaxed with his family, in his element
rough-housing with the kids. She was forced to
admit, yet again, that Gallagher was not the
philandering playboy type, for all that virile
masculinity he exuded. She realised that Gallagher
would make a wonderful father, a committed
family man. A funny twinge shot through her at
the thought.

She could see that Gallagher came by his
somewhat old-fashioned and traditional values
honestly, because after dinner the 'womenfolk' all
banded together to attack the dishes. His sisters
and his mother were all the epitome of femininity,
and she was beginning to understand why
Gallagher had had such problems accepting a
woman in a traditionally male role. Still, she joined
them, and actually had fun.

When they had finished, she realised that she
had not seen—or heard—Kenny for some time.
She scoured the house for him. No Kenny.

A dreaded vision of him wandering off into the
woods by himself crowded her mind. She saw

Gallagher. 'Have you seen Kenny?'

'He's doing me a favour.' Gallagher frowned at her anxious expression, lightly touched her knitted brow. 'Do you worry about him constantly?'

'Yes,' she said stiffly, stepping away from him. There, she thought. It was happening, just as she had known it would. He had known Kenny only a few days. Already, he was not accepting of the reality—that being responsible for Kenny took an emotional commitment, exacted an emotional toll.

Gallagher gave her a puzzled look, and then was gone. A few minutes later she heard the tinkle of sleigh-bells, and looked out of the window to see Gallagher leading the giant, gentle horses through the snow. Waving from the sleigh was Santa Claus.

A loud 'ho-ho-ho' brought the children scurrying to the windows, squealing their delight. Santa Claus entered the house with Gallagher behind him.

Charlie forgave Gallagher for his thoughtless slip of a moment ago. It was Kenny in the red suit and beard, and he played his role with fervent enthusiasm, beaming with pleasure at his importance.

After everyone had had a turn with Santa, they all went to change clothes, and then trooped outside to the sleigh.

Gallagher pulled her into the shadow of the house.

'Let's go for a walk, instead. We won't even be missed.'

'Kenny might wonder what's become of me. I should just——'

Again she saw a faint look cross his eyes. Or had it?

'I already told Ken we wouldn't be joining them.'

'You did, did you?' She arched a stern eyebrow up at him.

'Sometimes, there's only one way to deal with a stubborn woman,' Gallagher declared. He picked her up and tossed her over his shoulder.

Charlie was so surprised that a shout of laughter escaped her. She pounded helplessly on the small of his back with her fists. He ignored her, strolling effortlessly out into the woods beyond his house.

Finally, he put her down, and extended his hand. Wordlessly, the laughter still bubbling within her, she took it. She walked with him, and felt a wonderful peace begin to sneak up on her. It was quiet, save for the muffled sound of their footsteps and the far-off tinkle of sleigh-bells. The world was glorious, moon-washed to tones of silver and black.

They arrived at a ramshackle bench which was located under the drooping branches of a snow-laden pine tree. Gallagher brushed off the snow, and they sat down.

'Sorry for the caveman routine.' She could hear the smile in his voice. 'It was just something I had to get out of my system, before I said goodbye.'

'Goodbye?' she whispered, her voice strangled. So, this was it, after all. He had decided they couldn't continue working together——

'To the caveman,' he interrupted her whirling thoughts. The silence thickened around them before he spoke again.

'You know, the other day, when I mentioned rules to you, I think it was the first time I'd ever acknowledged their existence myself.'

'The man-woman rules?'

He nodded. 'I've been thinking about them ever since. You know, since Syn died, my relationships—if they could even be called that—have all felt hollow, boring. I thought it was because I still missed Syn.

'But I don't think that's it. It's because of this game everybody plays, myself included. At first the women I meet are so sweet and helpless and accommodating. And at first that feels good. It makes me feel like a real man. She needs me to look after her, she looks up to me. But then it starts to shift.

'Suddenly, I'm the centre of somebody's universe. Always expected to make the decisions. Always expected to make life fun and exciting. And before too long it starts to feel like a cage. It starts to feel cloying. And dead and dull. I think it's because nothing real is happening. Everybody's just playing their part, their role.'

He stopped, studying the night. His voice was very soft when he started to speak again. 'Then, someone genuine comes along—who doesn't play by the rules, who doesn't fit nicely into their allotted role. And, strangely enough, that doesn't feel good, either. It makes me feel bloody threatened, in fact. But it's never boring—there are times when it seems like it could be the most exciting thing that ever happened.

'If I let it. If I can let go of my need to always be the one with the answers, to always be the strong one. I guess I never thought of a relationship in terms of equality before. And now it seems I can't think about it in any other terms at all. Anything less than a man and a woman who can be totally real around each other seems like an empty sham. Anything less than a person I can share with totally, respect totally, be challenged by totally, doesn't seem like it would be worth having. Am I making any sense, Charlie?'

Well, he was making sense, but was he telling her a philosophy, or was he saying this applied to her? To her and him, together?

'You're making sense,' she offered cautiously, 'but I'm not sure where you're going.'

He laughed. 'I'm not sure where it's leading, either. Or if I'm even on the right track. I just know I don't want what I accepted as a relationship any more. I want it to be deeper and stronger. It may not always feel better but, dammit, it always feels alive—like it's going to change and grow endlessly, not wither and die, strangled by its own traps and pretences.'

'Are you talking about us, Gallagher?'

'Dammit, yes! I'm not sure what's going on between us, Charlie. Never have been, not from the first day. But I want to find out. Just one step at a time. Will you let me get to know you?'

'Yes,' she said simply. She knew she was finally allowing risk to come into her life. It didn't seem as scary as she had anticipated it would. It felt right. It felt so beautifully right.

They walked some more, talked some more. In the distance they could hear Christmas carols drifting over the night air. Finally, shivering with cold, they rejoined the others at the house.

The children were put to bed, and the adults gathered around the fire to sip eggnog, and roast chestnuts. Kenny fell asleep in the big wing-chair beside the fire, and one by one the others stretched and said their goodnights.

Gallagher's eyes caught on hers, and he moved from his chair to the seat beside her on the sofa.

'I should go,' she said, without much conviction.

'There's a guest-room upstairs for you, if you want to stay. Kenny can have the couch.'

It sounded so good. She was pleasantly exhausted, and not looking forward to the drive home. 'Thank you.'

'Merry Christmas, Charlie James,' he said softly, and a finger found its way to her hair, and traced a glittering strand downwards.

She returned his gaze, and longing erupted inside her. For his kiss. For more than his kiss. For a life of sitting in front of fires with him. For a life of being his partner and his soul-mate. A life of Christmas celebrations just like this one. A life of being the one he shared his dreams with, of his

being the one she shared her dreams with. A life of
sharing his bed. His heart.

'Gallagher,' she whispered. Her hand reached
out and touched the firm line of his lips. She knew
the truth in an instant—that she loved him, and
that it felt wondrous to love. Like a gift—like her
very own Christmas gift—from the heavens.

She leaned forward, intending only to brush her
lips across his. Intending only to cherish this gift
for one brief moment in time. She was aware that,
for all his words tonight, for all that she was
willing to take the risk, in the back of her mind
lingered the thought that life would catch up with
her.

His hand found its way to the back of her neck,
and the kiss became more than a brush—it became
a lingering exploration. His other arm came down
and wrapped around her, and she felt herself
being pulled into the hard wall of his chest. She
was beyond a point where she could have voiced
objection. It would have been like asking someone
dying of thirst to back away after only one taste of
cool, refreshing water.

His lips were like wine, though, not water. They
had their own flavour and texture and, like wine,
one small sip enticed yet one more. She
unhesitatingly drank of his heady wine, letting
herself explore and be explored, feeling the beat of
his heart against her breast, smelling the aroma of
hay and horses and chestnuts that clung to him.

His tongue parted her willing lips, and slipped
into the hollow of her mouth. What had been

gentle became more urgent—a summer breeze heralding the coming of a storm. It had whispered softly at first, but now it was increasing in tempo, the soft whisper turning into something stronger, more intense, more electrifying. She felt herself being swept willingly into the eye of the storm, riding on rolls of thunder, quaking as each of his kisses ripped through her like a lightning strike ripping through an indigo sky.

His lips left hers, and scattered kisses like hard raindrops over her upturned face. He anointed her eyelids and forehead, her cheekbones, the tender hollow of her throat. She was quivering now, like one who had indeed been caught in an unexpected onslaught of wind and rain. She did not feel cold, but white-hot, the fingers of heat flashing through her, touching here, touching there, until her whole being was on fire.

It was a torrential downpour—but not of rain. Fire. Painful, exquisite, searing fire. She ignited, her lips seeking the heated surface of his skin—flame meeting flame, touching tentatively, reaching out, mingling, dancing back, like some exotic African rite of passage. The flames teased and played, leaping together, surging, in each intricate motion moving closer to the joining, the melting . . . moving closer and closer to the one act that would finally, exultantly, extinguish the fire that grew so intense it was impossible to tell whether this raging heat was pain or pleasure.

'Charlie,' he moaned, his voice husky and tormented. 'Oh, Charlie.'

She lifted his head from her breast, looked deep into the sapphire eyes—eyes as clear and deep as a mountain lake. She saw in those eyes the promise that he would flow over her, smothering the fire gently, soothingly. It would be like slipping into a cool, tranquil pond on the hottest of summer days.

'Come to my room,' he murmured, nipping her ear.

'Yes,' she replied simply. 'Oh, yes.' There were no other words in her vocabulary at that moment. Intellect and reason had fallen swiftly, been swept away by the fire-storm of emotion, of pure physical need that raged within her.

His arms locked around her and he lifted her, setting her gently on her feet. She wrapped her arms wantonly around the strong column of his neck, pressed herself against his hard length, and then opened her eyes, wanting to drink of him, to let each of her senses act greedily, to let each of her senses have its feel of this wondrous storm.

But she saw Kenny, sleeping in the wing-chair, his chin dropped on to his chest.

'We should cover him,' she said softly, reluctantly. She felt instantly resentful of this small intrusion, this lull in the storm, this reminder of reality. And then ashamed of her resentment.

Gallagher sighed heavily, let her go. 'I'll get a blanket.' She could tell that he, too, resented reality. *And probably always would*, she thought dully. He left the room and her intellect tumbled back in force, as if annoyed that it had been held in abeyance for so long.

'Oh, lord,' she murmured, and sank wearily on to the couch. She noticed that the buttons of her shirt had come undone and, with a blush burning in her cheeks, she quickly redid them.

She couldn't go to his room with him. Kenny was here. Good lord, his mother was here! She did not want to be discovered tangled in his arms in the early-morning light. Even less did she want to sneak away from him after the loving, as if it were a criminal act, a thing of shame.

He came back into the room, tossed a quilt over Kenny, then turned to her. The fire flickering in his eyes died, and his shoulders heaved.

'You've changed your mind,' he said flatly.

She nodded miserably. 'Gallagher, I'm sorry. But I can't. I just can't.' Her gaze shifted to Kenny, and then back to him, prepared for rage, beseeching him to understand.

He came and sat beside her. 'You're right,' he said reluctantly. 'It's neither the time nor the place. We deserve more. I don't ever want you to feel guilty about anything that happens between us. I don't ever want it to be tainted by anything that could make it ugly. The time and the place will come, Charlie.' His voice was low, intense, and so firm.

She stared at her hands, not daring to look in those eyes for fear that reason would once again abandon her. Reason that calmly ticked off point after point why hope could be such a dangerous thing. His words tonight had been compelling but, by his own admission, he wasn't quite sure what he felt, or where it would lead them, or what he wanted.

'I think maybe I'll go home after all,' she said. She reached over and gave Kenny's shoulder a firm shake.

Getting a sleepy Kenny ready to go took a miserably long time, particularly with Gallagher watching silently. *Disapprovingly*.

Finally, they were ready to go. Gallagher handed Kenny a brightly wrapped package. He had nothing for her. For as little as he had really said tonight, had she even read too much into that? Surely, if he cared about her at all, he would have managed some sort of little gift?

'I have got something for you,' he told her softly. 'Next week.'

She cringed, wondering if her doubts and her childish disappointment had shown in her face. But the look he was giving her very foolishly made both her doubts and her disappointment fade.

He leaned forward and gave her a chaste kiss on the cheek.

Kenny snickered.

CHAPTER NINE

CHARLIE finished her schedule without the promised Christmas gift being produced. She knew it was childish to care. She knew it was puerile to feel put out every time Cherry and Rob flounced by in the bright red toques and scarves with 'High Heaven' embroidered on them. Presents from Gallagher, just like the set he'd given Kenny.

She didn't care about the gift, *per se*, she told herself fiercely. She cared about broken promises. This was broken promise number two for Gallagher Cole. He'd promised to include her on a ski trip, and never mentioned it again; he'd promised her a Christmas gift and never produced it. He seemed so damned reliable about everything else, to everyone else.

'Your face will freeze like that.'

She finished securing the tail rotor with a tie-down strap, refusing to look at his impudent grin.

'You're off for a while now, aren't you?' he asked casually.

Broken promise number three, if the words he had spoken on Christmas Eve could be looked at as a promise. She was beginning to feel as if she had misconstrued what he had said, made it up, imagined it.

Though things had been better between them.
No, not just better. Like night to day. He'd been
wonderful to be with this last couple of weeks.
Gentler. More vulnerable. Good-humoured.
Caring. She had really felt she was beginning to
see the authentic Gallagher. And she liked him.
No, that was an understatement—so much of an
understatement that it bordered on being a lie.

But now he was casually wishing her goodbye,
as if it didn't matter to him that he wouldn't see
her for two weeks. What had happened to 'Will
you let me get to know you?' It wounded her
pride, and raised her caution, that she seemed to
be feeling more—much more—than he was.

'Why don't you join us for dinner tonight?'
Gallagher asked. That look was in his eyes. That
look that made her believe in him all over again.

'That sounds good,' she said, hoping her voice
sounded faintly cool, and not at all shaky with
anticipation. 'Of course, I'll have to check with
Tanya and see if she wants to come over tonight.'

'Charlie, don't do that. Let Ken stay by himself.'

She felt her heart fall. She didn't want his
guidance on matters concerning Kenny. His
implication that she was overly protective. Not
doing things right. It threatened all her hopes and
dreams for them.

'We'll see,' she said, aware that her voice held a
frigid note that warned he was in territory where
he was not welcome.

He ignored the frigid note. 'For heaven's sake,

Charlie, give him some credit. He's not going to burn the house down, or have a wild party.'

How do you know? she wanted to shout. 'We'll see,' she said again, coldly.

Gallagher sighed. 'Well, call me when you're done "seeing".'

She surprised herself when she got home. 'How would you feel about staying home alone tonight, Kenny?'

'OK,' he said, not turning from the TV.

He obviously did not grasp the import of what she was asking. She turned off the TV.

'What would you do if there was a fire?'

Kenny rolled his eyes. 'Phone the fire department, course.'

'Where would you find the number?'

He looked at her as if she were a child. It was insulting. She wondered how often she looked at him like that.

'The number's in the phone.'

'In the phone?' she asked, her heart sinking.

"Member? When we moved here, we bought the phone that remembers numbers. Tanya and me put in a bunch. Fire is the red button.'

Charlie stared at Kenny, and then began to smile.

'. . . if there had been a fire,' she told Gallagher a little while later, taking a sip of her white wine, 'I would have been the one racing around frantically to find the phone book. Kenny would have calmly pushed the red button on the phone.'

She had terrific fun that night. They had a

sumptuous dinner, and then went and listened to a comedian, and played some pool. But most of the fun, she knew, was being with Gallagher. Though they were with a group of people, he had a way of looking at her and laughing with her that made it feel as though they were alone in the world. He listened to her. Really listened. And talked to her. Really talked. They were discovering ever so slowly that they shared a depth of feeling that set them aside from the rest of the world. It made their earlier differences seem shallow and superficial, so strong was this thing they shared.

It was an early evening, as Gallagher and the skiers had to be up at the crack of dawn the following day. Gallagher drove her home and walked her to the door. He did not attempt to kiss her, only watched until her key was inserted safely in the door, and then gave her a jaunty wave and went back down the path.

She slipped inside, closed the door and leaned on it, admitting that she was a bit dismayed at the lack of a kiss. It was true that the passion that she and Gallagher felt had a way of igniting, and might prove an obstacle to them getting to know each other on other levels, but certainly it was acceptable for even the most platonic to say farewell with something! A harmless peck on the cheek, or a lingering handshake.

She sighed, then realised that she was standing there with her eyes shut for more reason than the fact that she hadn't been kissed. She was actually afraid to open them and see what mischief

Kenny had wreaked upon the house. For that matter, where was Kenny? He never went to bed on his own.

She opened her eyes. The house was immaculate. In far better shape than when she had left. She could smell popcorn, and went into the kitchen, bracing herself to find burned pots and melted butter all over. The kitchen, too, was immaculate, the clean popcorn pot left upside-down in the sink to dry. She realised that she hadn't even known that Kenny knew how to make popcorn.

She went upstairs. Kenny was in bed, fast asleep, his clothes folded neatly on the chair beside him. Even the bathroom had been left tidy, without the usual toothpaste smears on the mirror and the sink.

She contemplated all this as she got ready for bed. She knew that Kenny had left her a message—rewarded her for trusting him, tried to tell her he was ready and able to be more independent. For some reason it depressed her. He was ready. Was she? And she couldn't even bring herself to dwell on that question long enough for an answer to come.

On her second day off, the phone rang. She recognised the deep baritone of Gallagher's voice immediately, and her heart did a joyous little jig.

But Gallagher had not called to ask her out, hadn't remembered that long ago promise to take her skiing, wasn't checking for a convenient time to drop off her Christmas present.

'Could you come to work tomorrow?' he asked brusquely.

'Sure. I guess so.'

'Great. See you then.'

'I'm fine,' she muttered to the dead receiver. 'And you?'

The next morning, when she pulled up to the hangar, there was no sign of Gallagher and no sign of the ski-buses. What there was was Leon, the other pilot, doing checks on *her* helicopter.

She got out of the car, and walked slowly over to him. She had assumed he was ill.

Leon turned and looked at her, gave her a winning grin.

'So you're the big date.' He studied her with embarrassing interest, and then let out a low whistle. 'This is probably going to cost Gallagher a couple of thousand. I'd say you're worth every penny of it.'

'I don't know what you're talking about. I'm nobody's date. Gallagher asked me to come to work today. Obviously he's got a mix-up on his hands. But, since you're the one scheduled, I'm going home.'

'Whoa there, Charlie,' Leon said, grabbing her arm when she turned away. 'Gallagher would kill me if I let you get away. He's probably going to kill me, anyway.' He pointed to a mess of ribbon and wrapping paper just inside the door. 'I was supposed to gift-wrap the interior.'

'Whatever for?'

'I think it's your Christmas present.'

'The helicopter?' she asked incredulously.

'A day in it, anyway.'

Charlie sighed. 'Would you please tell me what you're talking about?' Some gift. As if she didn't already spend every day in the helicopter as it was!

'Gallagher cancelled his skiers this morning. We only had one group. He found room for them with another company.' Leon looked over her shoulder. 'Here's the man of the hour, now.'

She turned to see Gallagher getting out of a bus. His arms were loaded with ski equipment and packages.

'Gallagher,' she implored him as he came up and dumped his load at her feet, 'what is going on?'

He picked up a pair of boots. 'Seven and a half. Your size?'

She nodded mutely.

He threw her a pair of ski-pants. 'Eight. Your size?'

She nodded again. Skis, poles, gloves, a toque, and sun-glasses were loaded into her arms.

'Gallagher——'

'Merry Christmas, Charlie. Ken conspired with me. He found your sizes in some stuff of yours at home.'

'I'm still not quite following. What . . .'

He paused, and looked at her, a slow smile spreading across his features. 'This is part one of a two-part Christmas present. I'm taking you skiing.'

Emotion rose in her throat so rapidly, she was

sure she was going to shame herself by bursting into tears. Quickly, she marched by Gallagher, and into the hangar to change into her gear.

Within minutes they had arrived at a gentle bowl that she recognised as a beginner-to-intermediate slope. They were dropped off, and she put on her skis, allowing memory to flood her. It had been so long. She wondered if she could really even manage in the deep powder. The helicopter departed. So did her doubts. This day, this experience, was brand new. Nothing could have ever been like this, and nothing would ever be like this again.

She and Gallagher stood shoulder to shoulder in the awesome silence, lost in a place without time, surrounded by diamond-crusted snow, by mountains, by endless blue sky. She lifted her face and felt the sun breathe its healing warmth into her, warm her through to her soul.

Gallagher suddenly pushed off, leaping forward, cutting smooth 'S's in the snow, leaving foaming powder in his wake. He stopped, waved at her. His smile was warmer than the sunshine—and had the same effect on her soul.

Tentatively, she shoved off, made a few experimental turns. Her knowledge came back to her slowly, even if it had to be applied differently to waist-high powder. By the middle of the first run, she was able to sail down to Gallagher, and cut a clean stop that left him doused in snow. He was off again, before she had time to catch her breath.

By their final run of the morning she was feeling confident. She ski'd slightly behind Gallagher, just over his right shoulder. They swept down the mountain like powerful birds in graceful flight.

She could feel something building in her as the wind tousled her hair and touched her cheeks, as the sun warmed her, as the snow shot out from under the sharp edges of her skis. Her legs burned from the unfamiliar exertion, but the burn was far away, overpowered by that something that built and built and built within her.

She became an eagle, soaring and swooping, doing a joyous dance with the earth, the elements, the sky. She was not a passive observer in a beauty so wild and untamed that it seemed to surpass anything a mere mortal was capable of longing for. She was a part of it. She was free. As free as the mountain, the wind, the sun, the snow. She was an equal partner with all these things. The world was a playground designed only for her delight.

They came over the final rise, saw the helicopter waiting in a hollow far below them, and raced towards it. She heard a sound. At first she thought it was a variation of the melody of the breeze. But it wasn't. It was laughter. Her laughter, spilling out of her, joining the symphony of the mountain. A whoop rose from within her, a shout of joy and exhilaration She heard Gallagher's answering shout, his laughter. She knew joy. She knew joy as she had never, ever known it. It raced around her, like wind, teased her, settled in her heart and her soul, enveloped her completely in its tender wings.

They stopped, breathless, at the helicopter.

Her laughter-filled eyes met Gallagher's. 'It's a good day to die,' she intoned solemnly.

He nodded his agreement, his eyes drinking in her face with wonder. 'A very good day to live,' he added softly.

Leon brought piping-hot lunch out of the helicopter, then set it, a blanket, and a bottle of wine in the snow. He waved at them and took off. Gallagher and Charlie planted their skis in the snow, spread the blanket at the base of them to sit on, and then used the skis as back-rests.

They tucked into barbecued chicken and sipped chilled white wine.

'I want to tell you about Syn,' Gallagher finally said quietly.

'Sin?' Charlie nearly choked on a chicken-bone.

'Synthia. The woman I was engaged to.'

Charlie nodded. 'I'd like to hear about her.'

'She left me the helicopter. Did you know that?'

'No,' Charlie responded softly, noting the faraway look in his eyes.

'Her family was in the business. They did heli-skiing as a winter sideline. That's how I met her. When she died, her dad told me that he'd named each of his helicopters after one of his kids, and Syn had specifically requested that, if anything ever happened to her, she wanted hers given to me. That's what I meant a long time ago when I told you there was more than one way to beat death.'

Charlie felt a painful fist squeeze her heart. 'You meant that Syn is still alive for you, up here? That you still have a dream together, even if you're doing it alone?'

He shook his head slowly. 'I think that's what she wanted, Charlie. To stay alive for me, to still be responsible for my every happiness. When I think about her now, it makes me sad. Really, all we had in common was a passion for the deep powder. I think it filled a lot of gaps in our relationship. I don't know if it would have been enough to sustain a marriage.

'Syn liked making other people happy. Especially me. Her happiness depended on my being happy. I liked it at the time. Loved it. Being adored, pandered to. But, in retrospect, I see a twist in it.

'People can't really *give* you happiness. You own your own joy. It's inside you, or it's not real. Syn's wasn't real, because it relied totally on me. I think that would have caused some problems for us.

'I guess what I'm saying is this—that I can't make *you* responsible for how I feel, for my happiness or my unhappiness. I'm responsible for myself. Knowing that is what makes me healthy enough and whole enough to think about getting into a relationship. A relationship based on freedom. Freedom to never have to try too hard. Freedom to be ourselves, to enjoy each other as people, rather than crippling each other with price-tags and expectations.'

Charlie gazed at him, startled and warmed by

his depth, his unexpected wisdom, his insight into life. 'I agree,' was all she said.

He returned her gaze, took her hand and gave it a hard squeeze. 'This day is yours and mine. Nobody else's. Maybe this life is yours and mine, Charlie. Nobody else's.'

The chopper was above them, and would have drowned out her answer, if she had had one. Her heart was in her throat. She loved this man. But hadn't he forgotten something? Forgotten that there was somebody else?

They ski'd only a few runs in the afternoon. Charlie was worn out. But the magic had faded, too. Because, she acknowledged, that had been inside her. And now what was inside her was a nameless dread. He had insinuated there might be a future. But for them. *Nobody else*. Had he forgotten Kenny? Or dismissed him?

She thought he must have. But then he leaned in her car window, after practically carrying her soaked and aching body to her car. He kissed her on the nose, a tenderness in his eyes that she had been dying to see, and yet now felt as though it were indeed killing her softly.

'Part two of the present,' he reminded her.

'What's that?'

'We've only got one group in right now. Nothing that Rob and Cherry can't handle. When's the last time you had a few days all to yourself? To sleep in, or sit on the couch all day and read, or to sip wine in the bathtub?'

She laughed tiredly. 'I don't think I've ever had

a few days like that.'

'That's my gift. I'm going to take Ken out to my place for a few days. He can help me replenish the wood-pile. And you are going to treat yourself to a few wonderful, carefree days on your own.'

'No!' she said sharply and instinctively.

Gallagher regarded her with unsettling intensity. 'What are you afraid of?' he asked softly.

'Nothing,' she responded emphatically, but it wasn't true. She was afraid. She was foggily aware of a dragon lurking in the shadows of her mind.

'Then it's settled?' Gallagher asked smoothly.

'I'll have to ask Kenny if he's interested,' she said without enthusiasm, hoping against hope that he wouldn't be. But of course he was, and he leapt at the chance to spend time alone with Gallagher.

Charlie found herself facing three empty, lonely days, wishing Gallagher had had the sensitivity to invite them both out to his place. But actually the days proved to be anything but empty, and, though she spent them alone, she did not feel lonely. It was on the third day that she acknowledged the fact that she was having fun—trying hard not to, but having fun, none the less. She slept in. She ate peanut butter sandwiches, and experimented with gourmet creations that Kenny always turned his nose up at and refused to eat. She sipped white wine in a bubble bath. She went shopping for *herself*. She never turned on the TV or the radio, appliances that were running constantly, and usually together, when Kenny was at home. She luxuriated in the silence, breaking it only with the classical records that she seldom listened to because Kenny complained so much at having to hear any kind of music that was not rock and roll.

Why had Gallagher done this for her? she allowed herself to wonder on the final day. Why had he done this *to* her? The ugly thought occurred to her that maybe he was starting to prepare her for a suggestion that she should make other plans for Kenny. Maybe he was trying to slowly wean her of her affection for her cousin, for his own purposes. Maybe he was trying to remove what he perceived as an obstacle to their relationship going anywhere.

No, she thought, Gallagher wasn't devious. But what if he was doing it at a subconscious level, without even realising what he was doing?

Suddenly, without warning, the dragon was there—huge and ominous—breathing a tortuous flame at her. She could not face the questions it asked of her.

Gallagher dropped off an exuberant Kenny later that afternoon.

'Did you have a good time?' he asked her at the door.

'Not particularly,' she lied, tempted to slam the door in his face.

'I thought I was doing something nice for you,' he told her testily.

'Well, from now on, keep your niceness to your damn self!' she snapped, and was immediately sorry when hurt and bafflement leapt in his eyes.

'Gallagher, I'm sorry. I didn't mean that.'

He regarded her thoughtfully. 'What do you want, Charlie?'

'I don't know,' she whispered. But that wasn't true. She knew exactly what she wanted. *Everything*. She wanted everything.

Oddly enough, over the next few weeks, that felt like exactly what she had. Everything. She joined the skiers on nights out more often, nights that always seemed to end up being for her and Gallagher. Nights that cemented the strong feelings that they had for one another. Nights of laughter and long talks and aching kisses.

On other nights, Gallagher asked Kenny to join the group for sleigh-rides and toboggan-rides. Several times, Kenny, at Gallagher's invitation, went up in the helicopter with them. Several times, Gallagher came and spent a quiet evening at her house, watching the fire, playing Monopoly. Everything. She took it all. While it lasted. While she could. Waiting for the bubble to burst.

Then one night she arrived at Gallagher's to find the normal crowd of people missing. They were alone.

'Where is everybody?' she asked softly, knowing now why Kenny had not been included in tonight's invitation.

'I cancelled the sleigh-ride. I think you and I have more important things to discuss.'

'Oh?' she asked lightly, though her heart was throbbing painfully in her chest. 'Like what?'

He poured her a glass of wine, handed it to her,

chinked his glass lightly against hers. 'Like you and me. Like where we're going. When we're going to get there.'

She put down her wineglass. 'I'm scared of questions like that, Gallagher.'

He touched her downcast cheek. 'I know you are. I am, too.'

'Well, then, why ask them? I'm happy—oh, lord, so happy—just the way we are.'

'No, Charlie. Life doesn't stand still. It grows. It changes.'

'I don't want it to,' she stated stubbornly.

He kissed her. Long and lingeringly, until she ached with a need to grow. To change. To know him. To know all of him.

He must have read each of these thoughts as they flickered across her face, because he smiled gently. 'Now tell me that you don't want it to change.'

She leaned back from him, and drank in the features of his face. The ruggedness was muted with tenderness, an unmistakably loving light lit the depths of those astounding blue eyes. She realised that the look he was giving her now was not new. She had seen that expression flicker through his eyes on and off many times in the past few weeks. She'd been baffled by it at the same time she had been warmed by it. But now she identified his expression as yearning. He wanted her. He loved her.

He pulled her close again, his warm, firm lips trailing tiny kisses over her upturned face. His lips erased her rational thoughts, her doubts, her anxieties. She was incapable of tainting this moment with worry about later. Gallagher drew her into the now, a wondrous place with no yesterday and no tomorrow, only moment upon precious moment, strung together like pearls on a golden thread.

'I love you,' she heard herself whisper.

He took her face in his hands, looked deep into her eyes with tender wonder. 'Now, when did that happen?'

'At the dawn of time,' she responded quietly, 'and it will last until the end of time.' Her honesty was frightening, but she met his eyes squarely. If he wanted something else, if he wanted only a temporary relationship, he would back off now—and she would crawl into a little hole, curl up in a foetal position, and die.

But he returned her intense gaze steadily. 'I felt it, too,' he said softly. 'The powerful tug of destiny, from that first moment I laid eyes on you. Only I didn't call it that. I called it trouble.'

She laughed, a sound that came from her throat like a contented purr. What she saw in his face was a man who was incapable of lying. Gallagher Cole could have his pick if he wanted to satisfy a brief urge. She had seen how women flocked to him, sensing in him that rare combination of power and playfulness, manliness and gentleness. But he had chosen her. Chosen her because she was his equal.

She firmly chased away the doubts that tried to crash into her serenity, that deep glow of contentment that was moving from her toes upwards. He was different. He was different from any man she had ever met. He had proved that he had more strength and more maturity than all the others. He didn't balk from realities. And he wouldn't balk from the reality that Kenny presented in their life.

And then that brief thought, too, was gone, chased away by lips that grew steadily more demanding, that commanded her to free herself of all but this—heartbeat matching heartbeat, heated skin meeting heated skin, hungry lips devouring hungry lips.

She was sand and he was ocean. At first he lapped over her gently, teasing, playing. But the waves grew in strength and intensity until she was finally swept up in a crashing, foam-crowned breaker. She found herself in his arms, sea-blue eyes washing over her.

'Tonight?' he said huskily, his voice holding both question and command.

'Tonight,' she agreed, and her lips fastened once again on his as he carried her up the staircase to his room.

She barely noticed the room, except to note that it was perfect. A fireplace dominated the far wall, a floor-to-ceiling window that looked out on a silver-washed world took up most of another. The bed was huge, yet inviting, with its handcrafted quilt of muted greys and golds and browns. He set her down on the bed, and she looked up through an enormous skylight at a velvet night sky embroidered with a zillion twinkling stars.

Gallagher came down beside her, capturing her lips again with an exhilarating urgency. Yet there was no urgency in the way his hands began their exploration of her. He moved slowly, stripping her clothes from her with such grace and sureness that she was barely aware of the transition—barely aware until his strong, dry hand traced the curve of her naked breast, moved with tender slowness over the flat plain of her stomach, and then dipped lower. She gasped with pleasure and need, arching against him. But he stayed her urgency, soothing her with his eyes and softly spoken words, even while he stoked the flame within her with his feather-light touch.

'Be still, love,' he commanded softly. 'I will know you.'

His mouth moved to trace the path that his fingers had mapped, and the shivers of delight and agony raced through her. His lips missed not an inch of her satiny skin; he anointed her from her eyelids to the tips of her toes.

The shivers were quickly becoming tremors, and she lifted his head once again to her lips and began an exploration not very different from his, eagerly seeking to know each portion of him—the firm, moulded chest, the iron-hard stomach, the steel of his inner thigh.

'Charlie,' he moaned.

'"Be still, love",' she commanded softly. '"I will know you".'

His firm, satiny skin began to ripple with

tremors of delight, tremors that grew in intensity until they rocked this mighty man.

She lifted her lips back to his, leaving her hair to dance over the surface of his muscled shoulders. His hand moved to both sides of her face and his lips accepted the invitation of hers, suddenly unfettered by tenderness, but fierce and commanding. She *was* his equal, even in this, and she came back to him, their tongues tangling, their teeth crashing against each other. His hands slid down the length of her, and up again, massaging with liquid fire, until she could feel the tremors within her building unbearably.

They were a volcano, now, building with steady, roaring tremors that rocked the earth. She could feel the inferno within her, white-hot lava boiling up, seeking the release only an explosion could give.

Eruption! And again eruption—and then slow shuddering amid the towering geysers of molten-red rock and white-hot ash that showered down around them. And then stillness, an awesome stillness, as the survivors clung to each other in the aftermath of nature's most magnificent demonstration of her power, of her beauty.

'Charlie,' he murmured against her hair. 'Beautiful, beautiful Charlie. How I love you.'

She was silent for a long time, stroking the sweat-glistening muscles of his back. 'So this is what you brought me here to discuss,' she finally teased throatily.

He hesitated, his discomfort like a brick wall

between them. 'In a way,' he said slowly, 'but this wasn't supposed to happen first.'

She felt a flicker of dread. 'What was supposed to happen first?' she asked with a casualness she did not feel.

'I wanted us to talk. About the future. About where we might be going. About things that have to be worked out between us.'

'Like what?' she asked, and now her voice was ice. She had been wrong. He wasn't any different from any other man. He wasn't going to accept her exactly as she was—or her circumstances exactly as they were. She had been a fool. She had overestimated him. On how many points about him had she allowed her emotion to cloud out her reason, cloud out the truth?

Still, a small part of her wanted so desperately to be wrong. Maybe, she told herself wildly, he wanted to know if she wanted a church wedding. Maybe he wanted to know if she wanted children. Maybe he wanted to know if she would continue flying after they were married. Married? She laughed harshly at herself. He had not mentioned marriage.

'I think you know what we have to talk about,' he told her quietly.

'Kenny,' she said dully.

He nodded, reached for her hand. 'Yes.'

She pulled the hand away from him.

CHAPTER TEN

CHARLIE jerked away from Gallagher, pulled the sheet around her, and sat up on the edge of the bed, feeling sick, feeling lost.

'What about Kenny?' she asked woodenly.

Gallagher tried to touch her, she stiffened, and he dropped his hand immediately. 'Look, maybe now isn't the right time.'

'Now is the perfect time,' she insisted coldly.

'What's wrong?'

'Nothing. Just say what you have to say, Gallagher.'

He sighed. 'Don't try and shut me out of one of the biggest parts of your life, that's what I'm trying to say. I want us to have a future, Charlie, but we have to sort out some things about Ken. We have to lay down some ground rules, now. If we don't, he'll be coming between us all the time. We'll be arguing about him all the time.'

'Is that right?' she said coolly.

'Look, Charlie, I know you're devoted to him. I admire you for it. But it's almost as though you're too close, and you can't see what's going on. You seem to overlook the fact that he's not a child. For heaven's sake, on Christmas Eve you tied his shoes for him!'

'It was late,' she said weakly and wearily. 'He was tired. It was easier to do that than to have him take three weeks to get them done up himself.'

'Charlie, he's a man! You wouldn't dream of tying my shoes for me, no matter what the circumstances. You have to try and stop treating him like a kid. Allow him some dignity. Let him grow up. Let him go!'

She had known that was coming. 'Go where, Gallagher?' she asked, in a soft, carefully controlled monotone. 'Go to a home somewhere, tucked away where he won't offend people, and won't interfere with normal lives like yours and mine?'

'That's not what I said,' Gallagher informed her tightly. 'You just said you loved me. Can you really think I'm that insensitive and callous, and claim to love me?'

'Then what are you suggesting?'

'How about a job? He's twenty-two years old, and you encourage him to play all day as if he were a little kid. He needs to have a place to go during the day, a reason for being. You should have seen him out here those few days that I had him. He was in his element.'

She turned and faced him, fire leaping in her eyes. 'You know it all, don't you, Gallagher? You've known Kenny for so long! And already you know what's best for him—or maybe,' she added acidly, 'what's best for you, where he's concerned. Well, once I thought he should work, too. But do you know the kind of work people like

Kenny are asked to do? Demeaning, boring things that they don't have to be paid a decent wage for because they're handicapped. People think that because they're mentally retarded they don't get bored, don't have to be shown their worth monetarily like ordinary people.

'In Calgary, I forced Kenny to go to a sheltered workshop. He sat around all day and snipped up rags. And then one day he took a shortcut through the alley behind the place where he worked. And what did he see in the garbage? The bags and bags of rags that he had blistered his hands cutting. The bags and bags of rags that he'd been paid two dollars a day to snip.

'He may be handicapped, but he isn't *that* stupid. He came home and cried. He cried non-stop for a week. He was ashamed. He wasn't so stupid that he didn't know that he lacked worth in the eyes of the very people who purported to be helping him. It took me almost a month to get him to go out of the house again. Work? You want him to work, Gallagher? At what?'

'It doesn't have to be like that,' Gallagher said softly.

'But how many times do I put him through that until we find the situation that isn't like that?'

'As many times as you have to, Charlie. Sitting at home twiddling his thumbs isn't doing any more for his sense of self-worth than cutting rags was doing. He wants to be like his friend Mike. He wants to have a job, an apartment, a girlfriend—a life.'

She turned and gave him a grim smile, then turned away and began untangling her clothes and shoving her leaden limbs into them.

'No, Gallagher, *you* want him to be like Mike. Isn't that the whole point? Get him a job and an apartment and a girlfriend, so you can seduce his cousin without worrying about him, without sharing your life with him. You want to care about him, but from a distance, like people who assuage their consciences by sending money to foster children overseas.'

'You're out of line,' Gallagher hissed coldly.

'Am I? Why don't you tell me the real reason you took Kenny for a few days?' she demanded, her voice shrill.

'The real reason?' Gallagher echoed, his puzzlement seeming genuine.

'You knew! You knew I'd have a wonderful time without him. You knew how much I'd resent him once he came back. You knew that, after that, all you'd have to do was tempt me and I wouldn't be able to resist life without him!' She paled, the impact of her words hitting her after they'd already come tumbling out of her mouth. She slammed a fist into her mouth, and bit it until the tears stung her eyes, but she could not clear the vision of the dragon, looming in front of her, breathing fire, scorching her to her soul.

'Oh, hell,' she murmured brokenly, and through her misted vision saw Gallagher rising off the bed, reaching for her, his face contorted with pain.

'Oh, hell,' she said again, and whirled from him, dashed out of the room, down the stairs, and into the cold night. A freezing night heated to an inferno by the breath of the dragon that pursued her.

'Chuck! You're late.' Kenny bounded into her room the next morning. He stopped, looked consideringly at her puffy eyes and pale face. 'You're sick.'

She nodded bleakly.

'I'll phone Gallagher. He's number three on the phone.'

She nodded numbly, staring at his disappearing back. Sobbed. He had spoken so decisively, with such authority. Like a man.

'He already knew you were sick,' Kenny told her a few minutes later. 'How'd he know?'

Charlie shook her head mutely.

'Tanya was going to take me cross-country skiing, but we'll stay and look after you instead.'

Again the decisiveness. And a somewhat startling act of sacrifice. 'No,' she managed to croak. 'Go. Please, go.'

He tried very hard not to look happy that his sacrifice had been refused. The house was empty and silent after he left. She stayed in bed—packing the contents of the house in her mind, crying, writing a letter of resignation in her head. Crying.

Gallagher had done this to her. She had to get away. Run away. Forget. She cried harder. No, Gallagher had not done this to her. The dragon had always been there, inside her. Waiting. There was no place to run. Not now.

Kenny came in that night. 'We didn't go skiing, after all. We went to the shop where Mike works.' His face screwed up with concentration. 'They have a new job to do. Putting things in envelopes. Little shampoos. And coupons. It's easy. I tried it. Simon's the boss. He said I could do it if I wanted. I said OK.'

She looked at him dully. Nodded. What else could she do? He didn't have to ask her permission. Why should he ask her permission? He was over eighteen.

'When I'm good enough at stuffing the envelopes, I can try the next station. Simon said . . .'

Charlie listened and didn't listen. For a week, she listened and didn't listen, the sadness spreading its tentacles throughout her like a weed taking root.

Kenny tried to be sensitive to her feelings, but he was too excited about his life. He talked with animation about the work he was doing, the people he was meeting. And the empty house each day made it that much harder to run.

She thought Gallagher might call. He did not. She grieved his loss, grieved it and yet knew, this time, she had no one to blame but herself. She had acted defensively, jumped to conclusions, accused him of things on an assumption that he was just like Paul. She knew better. She knew he was not like Paul, but it didn't matter. She couldn't have

Gallagher. He had talked once about relationships needing two people who were healthy and whole to make them work. She did not feel either healthy or whole. There was something within her that was ugly and terrible, and she could never have him while it was there. Nor did she have the strength to face it.

She took to watching game shows in the mornings, soap operas in the afternoons, and anything at all in the evenings, just so that her mind would stay numb. Once she wondered, as she turned on the TV in the morning, if this was the life she had given Kenny. It was awful. She hated it, felt powerless to do anything about it, and was glad that, despite her lack of encouragement, Kenny had managed to pull himself out of the mire she would have imprisoned him in for life.

'Chuck, Mike's room-mate moved.'

She glanced up from the TV and her depleted box of freezer Danish. 'So?' She didn't mean to use that tone with him, but she couldn't help herself. Nothing mattered any more, nothing but avoiding the dragon.

'He asked me to move in with him. I could do it, Chuck. I could. I make enough money. I'd have some left over for food. And enough for a movie once every two weeks. Simon, at work, helped me figure it out. And he said I could apply for——'

'No!' It came out as a scream, and she saw the shock register on Kenny's face. It was quickly followed by anger.

'I want to live with Mike,' he yelled. 'I want to

be a grown-up, like you. I want to have you and Gallagher over for supper one night, like Mike has Tanya and me sometimes.'

'Kenny, I'm sorry I yelled. I am. We can't talk about this right now. I can't.'

'Don't call me Kenny!' he screamed. 'I'm not a little kid! Nobody at work calls me Kenny.'

'Please. Not now,' she whispered. Not now, when I'm losing the one man in this world I can love. I don't want to lose you, too. Not in the same month. Not ever.

But Kenny was glaring at her. 'You don't love me, Charlie. You hate me. You hate me!'

She stared at him. She could feel the blood draining from her face. She found she wanted desperately to deny it, but could not. Her moment with the dragon had come.

She stood in the darkness, watching the cheery light from Gallagher's barn throw gold across the snow. It was beautiful, like a scene from a Christmas card. So many times, she thought, she had compared scenes in Revelstoke with scenes on Christmas cards. She wondered if that was why she liked it so much. Because she wanted life to be like a Christmas card, beautiful and pleasant, pretty scenes frozen in time.

She took a deep breath, walked to the slightly ajar door, and slipped in. She stood there for a moment, just watching, engrossed in yet another pretty scene. Gallagher was pitching hay to the horses, almost lost in the mist coming in great clouds out of their mighty nostrils. Despite the chill in the barn, he wore only faded jeans and a flannel shirt, the shirt-sleeves rolled up over the corded muscle of his forearms.

She could see his profile, and noted that there were weary lines etched around his mouth that she had never noticed before. Even in the dim light, she could see that he looked haggard and bleak, like a man who had not slept often or well.

'Gallagher.'

He whirled and looked at her, and her heart caught in her throat. His chest was heaving, his hair curling damply around his head from his exertion. He looked so strong and earthy and healthy, all things which she knew him to be. She knew she had done him a grave disservice to think he had any motive other than Kenny's welfare at heart that night two weeks ago.

'Hi.' His voice was non-committal. He turned back to his horses.

She moved to him, stroked a giant nose absently. She suspected that Gallagher was not a man who would forgive easily a lack of trust from one who had claimed to love him. She had not come to try and win him back, though, now that she was standing here, she wondered if that motive did not linger in her mind. She had only come to tell him about Kenny. Everything. She didn't know why. Maybe because she felt that Gallagher Cole had fallen in love with an illusion—a picture on a Christmas card. Maybe it would be easier to walk away from him knowing that once he knew the whole truth he would no longer feel the same for her. The love he had felt, she had felt, would be destroyed, as everything she loved was destroyed.

'I came to talk,' she said simply.

'I kind of guessed that.' Again, there was a note of uncaring in his voice. Because she had wounded him, or because he didn't care any more?

'Let me finish with the horses. We'll go to the house and have some hot chocolate.'

She nodded, but felt her courage fade as he worked silently on, not mentioning work, not talking to her at all. Why was she here? What difference did it make now? It looked like he had fallen out of love with her as naturally as he'd fallen in. Was there any reason to belabour the point?

He made hot chocolate as silently as he had fed the horses. He said nothing; he did not look at her. Even when he was seated in the chair across from her, he poked abstractedly at the fire.

'I want to tell you about Kenny.'

He shrugged. 'OK.'

She hesitated. Where to begin? Maybe at the ending, and work backwards. 'He got a job, Gallagher. He's moving out, too.'

Gallagher's eyes met hers for the first time, and she recoiled from the furious light she saw there. 'So, now that he's looked after, you don't have to worry about the ugly ogre interfering with his life? Shipping him off to a home at the first opportunity?'

She realised now that his indifference had masked a tremendous hurt. 'Gallagher, there was an ogre. But it wasn't in you. Maybe I just wanted to believe it was so I wouldn't have to look at myself. I had to look at myself, anyway.'

She stopped. She had promised herself she would not cry—because that would seem like pleading. She had promised herself she would just tell the story, all of it, and let the chips fall where they would. She had not a doubt that any feelings Gallagher had for her would be dead after her admissions. Maybe, she admitted honestly, that was the real reason for the tears that pricked behind her lashes.

'Kenny wasn't born like that.'

Gallagher looked up from the fire, startled. 'What?'

She shook her head, tried to smile. 'He was a perfectly normal little boy. More than normal. Hell, cute as a button, bright, inquisitive. When I first moved in with Aunt Joss and Uncle Henry, I was so thrilled with him. I made him my baby. I played with him. I insisted on being the one who fed him, changed him, put him to bed. He was the family I had always wanted so darn badly.' She was aware that her voice was beginning to shake, and fought to steady it.

'I did that to him,' she managed to blurt out, and then stopped, fighting for composure. 'I made Kenny the way he is today.'

The indifference was fading from Gallagher's face, but the look of shared pain he gave her only

increased her agony. She wanted him to love her.
Yearned for it. Perhaps if she left this story only
half-told—left out the dragon—he would love her
out of pure sympathy. The idea appealed
momentarily, and then she dismissed it. No, he
had to love her for exactly what she was. Anything
else would be a sham, a complete mockery of what
love was meant to be. But she knew it was a pretty
tall order she was looking for.

'He was two,' she said. 'We were out in the
yard. I was eight. I was supposed to be watching
him. I was. I was watching him. He was playing
on some steps. But I was also playing with my
dolls and the little girl from across the street. I
could see that he was eating something. I never
went and checked. I don't know, if I had, if I
would have known that he shouldn't be eating the
peeling paint——'

'Good lord,' Gallagher murmured. He was
getting up from his chair, but she stayed him with
her hand. Reluctantly, seeing her face, he sank
back down.

'It was a lead paint,' she said. 'Of course, they're
not entirely sure it was that, and nobody ever
blamed me, Gallagher. Ever. But I blamed myself.
Always. Every time I look at Kenny I wonder what
he could have been . . .' She took a deep,
shuddering breath.

'The dragon,' she said softly, 'the fourth dragon
is guilt, Gallagher.'

'The fourth dragon?' He was looking gravely
concerned now.

'Charlie James. There she goes. The saint. Dedicated. Devoted. Self-sacrificing. No, Gallagher, guilty. Trying so damn hard to absolve myself . . . absolve myself, punish myself. Yes, I fought his independence, but I fought it because I was afraid it would just explode a secret longing I harboured to be rid of him, to be free to lead a normal life. I guess I thought that if I pushed too hard for him to work, to live on his own, I thought he would know, the world would know.' She was sobbing into her hands. 'The truth, Gallagher. He knows, anyway. He thinks I hate him . . . and sometimes—sometimes, I'm not so sure . . .'

Now, she thought blearily, Gallagher would see all that she was. Not a pretty sight. And he would get up and walk away, and she would never blame him.

Except that he was beside her on the sofa, and he gently touched her shoulders, guiding her into the hard wall of his chest, stroking her hair as though she were a little girl who had just lost her puppy beneath the wheels of a car.

'You're one brave and beautiful lady, Charlie James,' he finally murmured softly.

'Brave?' She dared to peek up at him through swollen lids.

'It sounds like you just got yourself a dragon,' he said gently.

'Did you hear me?' she asked incredulously. 'Despise me, Gallagher! Despise me for the charade I've played out. Despise me for betraying a poor handicapped kid who relies on me. I despise myself.'

'Charlie, would your life be any different today if you hadn't been the one who was supposed to be watching Kenny that day? If it had been someone else who had turned their back for a moment?'

His words sank in, and the crazy roar inside her head slowed. 'Of course not,' she answered in a clear whisper. 'Of course not.' But then she could feel the roar picking up tempo again. 'But it doesn't change anything. Because it's not what happened then that makes me feel so angry sometimes. It's the fact that I can't come and go as I please. It's picking up after him, and yelling at him and constantly reminding him. It's cooking and doing laundry, and explaining things to him over and over again, and spending my days off at games arcades giving him quarters.

'It's the fact that I've made sacrifices for him that he can't begin to understand, let alone appreciate. I lost my youth to him. I lost a fiancé because of him. Do you hear me now, Gallagher? Do you hear what I'm saying?' She was crying again, uncontrollably, and once again he was unrepelled. He took her and cradled her against his chest.

'I hear exactly what you're saying. You love him very, very, much.'

'Gallagher, don't! Don't try and read things into me and this situation that just aren't there.'

'I've heard a story very similar to yours once before,' Gallagher said evenly. 'From my kid sister shortly after she had her first baby. She came to me weeping. She couldn't bear motherhood. She hated the constant demands. The feeding. The nappies. The never-ending loads of laundry. Getting up in the middle of the night. She resented her lost freedom; she hated the fact that her life would never be quite as free and easy again. And then she told me she was afraid she didn't even love her baby any more. I told her what I'll tell you—that's exactly what love is.'

'I'm not following,' Charlie admitted tremulously, but hopefully, and the hope drove back the roar.

'Don't you see, Charlie? You're human. You hate and resent the drudgery, but not Ken. You wouldn't do what you do for him if you didn't possess the most incredible of loves. Couldn't. It's the strength of your love that enables you to continue to do those things day after day, that makes you strong enough to do them. If it were really anything else, you'd just walk away and never look back. Maybe it's not the kind of love that poets are fond of talking about. It's not the firecracker variety. But it's the strongest kind of all. It's that steady, day-to-day kind of love that just keeps going, even when you want to give up.'

A dam burst within her, and the tears flooded down her cheeks, washing away the roar.

'I love him so much, Gallagher,' she finally choked. 'I thought you were going to make me choose. I didn't think I was strong enough to choose him, and that made me think I didn't love him at all.'

His eyes were gentle on her face. 'Do you love

me that much, too? That contemplating a choice I would never ask you to make would tear you to shreds like this?'

'Do you have to ask?' she whispered.

He smiled and lifted her chin. 'I only asked because I like to hear the words. I see the answer in your eyes. I'm awed. I'm honoured. Teach me, Charlie. Teach me this kind of love. Teach me how to give it back to you. Time is so short. Only a lifetime . . .'

She touched the curve of his proud cheekbone. 'You already know, Gallagher.'

'Yes,' he whispered, his voice husky against her hair. 'Yes, I know about loving you. But I have a feeling that every day I will learn more. Teach me, Charlie. Marry me.'

In answer, she scattered kisses as delicate as morning dewdrops across the rugged surface of that beloved face. In answer, she pressed her yielding body against the silk-sheathed steel of his. In answer, she wrapped her arms around him, let her fingers dance tenderly across the rippling muscles of his back. In answer, she whispered, her voice as soft as a summer breeze, 'Let's teach each other, Gallagher. Now. Right now.'

In answer, he scooped her off the couch, and laid her on the deep pile of the rug in front of a dying fire. In his eyes, in his lips, in the gentle lessons of his hands, were all her answers. For all time.

Afterwards, they lay tangled together beside the fire for a long time. There were no words; there was no need for words. Contentment rose up within her. Peace as she had never known it. Joy as she had not known it could be.

She thought maybe he slept, his arms wrapped around her as though he would never let go. But then his lips touched hers. It was a kiss that worshipped, and she opened her eyes to see him looking at her with muted intensity, looking at her as though he would never be able to see enough. She thought her joy had reached its bounds in his gentle and tender acceptance of her. All of her. Now she found that joy had no bounds.

His eyes left hers, and he buried his head in the richness of her hair. He spoke no words, but she felt the depths of his contentment. The joy swelled again within her as it met his, and mingled with his, swelling and swelling and swelling, joy without limit, without end.

And this was but a moment in a long line of moments that he offered her. Yes, she would marry this man. They would have children. Together they would explore heights higher than most people dared to contemplate.

Not that she expected moment upon moment of pure joy. No, she knew now that there were different kinds of love, and that they resided side by side. There was the kind of love that saw you through tedium and fights and quarrels. There was the kind of love you felt for your children, and the kind of love you felt in moments of passion, and moments of quiet. No, not so much different kinds. One love. One magnificent force with a zillion different manifestations of its power.

'Heaven,' she whispered and, unexpectedly, the tears started to flow down her cheeks. She had never cried with joy before this night.

'"You will know heaven on earth",' she said softly, quoting Tanya. And she did.

Charlie turned from the kitchen counter at the slamming of the outside door. Gallagher traipsed in, his boots carrying about forty pounds of snow and straw, mud and manure.

'Go take off your boots,' she ordered crisply.

'No,' he shot back.

She took in the firm set of the jaw, the wide sapphire eyes. He was tired and cranky, she realised. Too bad—she was tired and cranky, too.

'Right now,' she said with soft warning.

'Oh, all right,' he said grouchily.

He came back in and sat at the table. Charlie placed a cup of hot chocolate in front of him, and he slurped it noisily.

'I want to go to Kenny's house.'

'Gallagher, we've been through this already today. We can't. Ken is busy with his friends. He'll probably come out at the weekend.'

'With Helena?'

Charlie smiled. Helena. The chubby, fun-loving young woman Ken had met at work. He thought she was the most beautiful woman in the world. He didn't go very far without her these days.

'I think so.'

'Good. I like Helena.'

'Me, too,' Charlie agreed absently, putting the last neat row of chocolate-chip cookies on the sheet, and popping them into the oven.

'Can I have one of those?'

'They're not baked yet, Gallagher.'

'I want a cookie!' he screamed.

'Well, you're not getting one,' she screamed back, and was immediately mortified. Nobody had told her there were going to be days like this.

Gallagher threw his hot chocolate on the floor, and went down after it, beating his small fists on the rug. 'I want a cookie,' he yelled over and over again, splashing hot chocolate with each beat of his fists.

Charlie sighed, went over and picked him up off the floor. His hands snaked around her neck, and his sobs subsided.

'I'm sorry, Mommy,' he whispered. 'I love you.'

She moved into the living-room, sat in the big wing-chair. He was already asleep, nestled against her chest, one chubby fist tangled in her hair. Watching him sleep, she felt her nerves slowly relax, felt her aggravation being replaced with a luscious tranquillity.

'I love you, too,' she whispered, running her hand through the beautiful crop of dark curls that capped his head. She gazed at him, astounded, as she always was, by how much he resembled his father. The tranquillity spread its fingers inside her.

The house was dark when Gallagher came in. He

sniffed the air and dashed into the kitchen, opened the oven, and threw a sheet of charred cookies into the sink.

He turned to go in search of Charlie, and slid through something on the floor. He squinted down. Hot chocolate? Poor Charlie, he thought with a wry grin. Another one of those days.

She had cried about it yesterday. She cried quite a bit lately. From experience, he knew that was par for the course. And he knew that, right now, she just didn't have her usual energy with junior, never mind anything else.

'It's OK,' he'd told her yesterday. 'Let's not look back on our lives and be able to say we were perfect—at all the wrong things. Who cares if the house gets a little messy? Anyway, the season's almost over. I'll be home soon to help out. Gee, I've missed you up there this year, Chuck.'

The look in her face in that moment—her love as fresh as if they had only just met, when they'd been married and working together close to five years.

He wandered into the living-room and saw her. Gallagher was asleep on her chest, beautiful, thick lashes throwing shadows across his little round cheeks. He looked like an angel, which Gallagher Senior happened to know was not the case.

Charlie was asleep, too, her arms tight around the little boy, her face serene and untroubled. The fire was dying in the hearth behind them, and they were silhouetted in reds and oranges and golds.

He crossed the room on soft feet, and gazed

down at them. Charlie was just beginning to
show, he thought, feeling a stirring of fierce
protectiveness and intense love.

Unexpectedly, looking down at her, a lump
grew in his throat. He reached out and tenderly
touched the wild tangle of her hair, and felt a
strange prick behind his lashes. He took the
sleeping boy from her lap, and nestled him against
his shoulder, but he couldn't pull himself away
from her. He stood gazing at her, until finally the
light in the room died.

He turned slowly away to put Gallagher to bed.
Once, he remembered, he had asked her to teach
him of love. And she had.

And once, he realised, he had thought that the
closest he would ever come to heaven was when
he was waist-high in the deep powder of a virgin
slope.

And he had been wrong.

H A R L E Q U I N
Romance®

Coming Next Month

Available in January wherever paperback books are sold, or through Harlequin Reader Service:

In the U.S.
901 Fuhrmann Blvd.
P.O. Box 1397
Buffalo, N.Y. 14240-1397

In Canada
P.O. Box 603
Fort Erie, Ontario
L2A 5X3

In December,
let Harlequin warm your heart with the
AWARD OF EXCELLENCE title

Harlequin Presents...

PENNY JORDAN

a rekindled passion

Over twenty years ago, Kate had a holiday
affair with Joss Bennett and found herself
pregnant as a result. Believing that Joss had
abandoned her to return to his wife and child,
Kate had her daughter and made no attempt
to track Joss down.

At her daughter's wedding, Kate suddenly
confronts the past in the shape of the
bridegroom's distant relative—Joss. He quickly
realises that Sophy must be his daughter and
wonders why Kate never contacted him.

Can love be rekindled after twenty years?
Be sure not to miss this AWARD OF EXCELLENCE
title, available wherever Harlequin books
are sold.

HP-KIND-1

Harlequin Supperromance.

THEY'RE A BREED APART

The men and women of the Canadian prairies are slow to give their friendship or their love. On the prairies, such gifts can never be recalled. Friendships between families last for generations. And love, once lit, burns hot and pure and bright for a lifetime.

In honor of this special breed of men and women, Harlequin Superromance® presents:

SAGEBRUSH AND SUNSHINE
(Available in October)

and

MAGIC AND MOONBEAMS
(Available in December)

two books by Margot Dalton, featuring the Lyndons and the Burmans, prairie families joined for generations by friendship, then nearly torn apart by love.

Look for SUNSHINE in October and MOONBEAMS in December, coming to you from Harlequin.

MAG-C1R

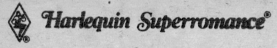

A powerful restaurant conglomerate that draws the best and brightest to its executive ranks. Now almost eighty years old, Vanessa Hamilton, the founder of Hamilton House, must choose a successor. Who will it be?

Matt Logan: He's always been the company man, the quintessential team player. But tragedy in his daughter's life and a passionate love affair force him to make some hard choices....

Paula Steele: Thoroughly accomplished, with a sharp mind, perfect breeding and looks to die for, Paula thrives on challenges and wants to have it all...but is this right for her?

Grady O'Connor: Working for Hamilton House was his salvation after Vietnam. The war had messed him up but good and had killed his storybook marriage. He's been given a second chance—only he doesn't know what the hell he's supposed to do with it....

Harlequin Superromance invites you to enjoy Barbara Kaye's dramatic and emotionally resonant miniseries about mature men and women making life-changing decisions. Don't miss:

- CHOICE OF A LIFETIME—a July 1990 release.
- CHALLENGE OF A LIFETIME—a December 1990 release.
- CHANCE OF A LIFETIME—an April 1991 release.